TO KNOW YOUR NAME

Tawnya Torres

ISBN-13: 978-1-958557-54-9

Fireheart Press
1477 Hanford Ave.
Lincoln Park, MI 48146
editor@whitecatpublications

PART ONE

My Name is Riku

CHAPTER ONE

Nothing Without You

My father is cross with me. Fine lines etch the corners of his eyes and mouth. I can't stand having this conversation with him again. No amount of words will make him understand.

"Riku, it is a privilege to lead. Why do you refuse it?" he scolds me.

"The others are better suited for this position," I say, trying to hide my irritation. A growl builds low in my throat. I snuff it out and put on a placid face.

"I don't want Rena or Ryo to be my successor. I choose you, Riku! " he bellows.

"Why me?"

Frustration causes me to clench my teeth and I taste blood.

"You are my best son. I need you to do this," he says, lowering his voice. My father does this in an attempt to seem humble. I laugh at his remark.

"I doubt Ryo would agree."

My older brother has had his eyes on the throne for decades. He resents me for being our father's favorite. If Ryo did become king of the northern demon wolf clan he would still resent me.

"I don't care what Ryo thinks he is entitled to!"

"I decline your challenge."

I bow as I walk backwards into the snow.

"Riku! Come back!" He keeps calling my name but I am in the wind.

***

For a thousand generations wolf demons have kept the tradition of fighting each other for the crown. My father fought his father and so on. Often these duels end in death. It's a custom I don't believe in. My loyalty is constantly questioned. Denying the challenge is a disgrace but I don't want to be his executioner. How can he ask this of me?

The only ones who don't pressure me to be king are my youngest siblings, the twins Yahei and Yuri. They have little interest in our family's brutality. Yahei puts on a brave face for our father but is clumsy and a bit of a coward. He would have more confidence if Ryo didn't belittle him every time they spoke. Yuri is bright but timid. Rena calls her a "rabbit" and ridicules her for not being more of a wolf.

My older sisters Yama and Rena are cold and distant. Yama treats me with indifference, we walk the halls like strangers. Rena is the eldest and most vicious. There have been other female wolf demon leaders but our father is a man of particular values. I have heard her argue with him over the advantages of a queen. Rena is fierce and persistent, there is no doubt she would make a fine leader. They are at each other's throats most of the time. It is because they are too alike. I can hear them fighting as I sneak through the castle.

"Why should it be Riku? He doesn't even want it!" Her voice echoes throughout the walls. They tremble, pierced by her harsh tone.

"I have already made my decision. We've been over this, Rena."

"I am just as strong as he is. Give me the challenge! I guarantee I can do it better and faster than he ever could," she growls back at him.

"You might have the power he does but you lack control. You have no discipline. When you transform you roam the world as a savage beast! What good are you to me then?"

Something goes flying across the room and hits the floor with a thud. It's true. During the last war Rena used her colossal wolf form. She slayed most of the army by herself but was lost to her demonic rage, resulting in the murder of our own men. Of course she was pardoned. It still brings our family shame. I try to avoid her but she spots me.

"Heavy weighs the crown, little brother. I don't think your puny shoulders can handle it." I don't say anything. This infuriates her more and she throws me into the wall. "I don't know what Father sees in you," her voice is raspy from all her shouting. She has plum colored lips, capable of chewing through bone and spitting venom.

"To be honest, I don't either."

This answer displeases her. Rena narrows her gray eyes at me. They hold nothing but fury and ice. She has sparse but long white eyelashes. Thin, dramatically arched eyebrows frame her indignant face. She pushes me against the wall and hisses in my ear.

"Take it, little brother. The throne is yours," she says and slams me down before stomping away. Her straight silky hair sways with her harsh movements.

"What if I refuse? What then?" I shout at her. She stops but doesn't turn around.

"Why do you fight your destiny, Riku? Do you wish to be ostracized?" Rena walks away without an answer. I wouldn't have been able to give her one anyway.

***

Winter is my favorite time of year. The snow on the mountain dulls the senses. It's easier for me to evade my family in the white abyss. I love them but I keep my distance. I wish to live my life for me. This is not a privilege wolves have. Everything is for each other. We recite the demonic canon daily, "The King is God. God is everything," we then put two fingers to our lips before pointing to one another, "Nothing without you." Our customs are strict and unusual. Striking down my aging father and resuming the throne doesn't seem dignified.

The river hasn't frozen over yet. I walk through it to cover my scent. Going against the current leads to a waterfall lined with rough boulders and cedar trees. The rushing water is loud but soothing. I climb the rocks until I get a third of the way up. Here is a cave, the spot where I go to think. Right now it's serving as my hiding place.

Living in that hollow castle leaves me resentful and agitated. It's colder in there than it is out here. I worry about Yuri. My sister is sensitive and smart. She is identical to our mother, Yuna, but they are nothing alike. Yuri is the smallest in our family. Frail arms, long neck, and thin body hold only the remnants of our mother's ghost. Her face is too fierce for her build. She has exhausted eyes with heavy lids. The pointed nose, thin eyebrows, and cherry blossom lips don't fit her sweet demeanor. They are pretty but poisonous. A combination of new and old.

In many ways I think Yuri is lucky to have lived most of her life without our mother. She was only a child when she died. Yuna's ruthless nature was worse than Rena's. My mother ripped out her father's heart to become queen of the southern demon wolf clan. It was ironic when a human's bullet tore through her chest, rendering her truly heartless.

"Riku! Come here, boy. I can smell you," Ryo shouts. I watch him wade through the river with his sword drawn.

"Stop this insolence and return to the castle," he's hacking away at the foliage as he talks. Whole ferns and branches float downstream.

"I know you can hear me so I'll inform you of Hoshi's arrival."

Ryo's grin is smug. Hoshi is the woman I'm supposed to marry. My father is insistent on keeping ties with our neighbors to the west, another tradition I don't believe in.

"Stupid, ungrateful whelp."

Ryo knocks the top off of a small sapling. He's pretending it's my head. Pivoting in the snow his gold eyes search for me. He gives the waterfall a once over and I swear he's paused where I am. Making no more effort to hunt me down he goes back the way he came. A gust of wind brings out the cold lurking in the sea of trees.

"See you at home," he calls.

His booming voice shakes the snow off the pines. Ryo and I look just like our father. Wolf demon's have wide set eyes, unlike the human's who have almond shaped eyes. We appear as foreigners. Our cheekbones are chiseled and sit high. My bottom lip is bigger than my top lip. Ryo says it makes me look permanently smug.

My brother and I have the same amber eyes, prominent chin, and hair the color of frost. He keeps his long and up as our father does. I cut mine short to spite them both. Rubbing the back of my head I remember pulling the hair to the nape of my neck and using my sword to take it off. I let it fall around my face and hang in my eyes. I wait for the sun to start setting before I head home. My brother's footprints have been lost to the fresh fallen snow. The sapling he cut down looks at me like it's my fault.

"Sorry," I say to the poor thing as I walk by. Ryo always left destruction in his wake. I can't remember a time when he wasn't terrorizing someone or something. It's getting late as I arrive at the castle. I'm greeted by Yahei.

"Riku! You're home." His face fills with relief.

"What are you doing out here?"

"Father and Hoshi's family are talking business."

He shrugs. I notice him grab his shoulder and wince in pain.

"What's wrong with your arm?"

"Today during my fighting lesson Ryo struck me. It's fine," Yahei admits but tries to sound tough. I feel my forehead crease but I keep my voice calm.

"You're doing great. I'll teach you next time," I say and pat his head. Ryo is always bullying Yahei. I try to protect him but I can't be around all the time. As soon as my boots hit the floor my father is there dragging me by the elbow.

"You knew she was coming today," he states.

"I forgot," I lie. My lies these days are countless and my father can't believe anything I say anymore.

"You are incorrigible," he says.

Gripping the crook of my arm with an angry fist he guides me to the tea room where Hoshi and her father are waiting. Hoshi smiles at me with no indication of annoyance. I feel bad avoiding her. She's been in love with me for years. Everyone knows she's too good for me. Except her. Her father doesn't look at me.

"Riku, where have you been?"

"My apologies. Riku has been helping our neighbors to the east," my father lies for me.

"I'm sorry, Hayao. It won't happen again," I say, even though it will.

"I hope you have fared well since I last saw you," says Hoshi. Her juniper eyes focus on me and I wish to disappear.

"Yes," I say, another lie. "Thank you, Hoshi. How were your travels?"

"They were promising. We have united the whole west coast," she beams.

"That's excellent news," I say.

I am a terrible son, brother, and fiance. Hoshi stands up to embrace me. She is a casual beauty. An airy face with a round nose that is pleasant on her. She has hair that is the color of the sun but her eyebrows and eyelashes are dark. I hold her but feel detached, like a ghost. I'm on the outside looking in.

"I missed you, Riku," she says. Our fathers are watching my every move. I pull her close and pick up a handful of her sunny locks.

"I missed you, too." I choke on my words.

CHAPTER TWO

The Darkness

I'm sparring with Yahei today. He is skilled with a sword and light on his feet but he lacks spirit. His strikes are strong but easy to predict. There is nothing wild about his attacks. Everything is proper procedure, no instinct.

"Try again."

"Riku, I don't think I can do this."

"Yes, you can," I say.

"But I don't understand what you're trying to teach me. Maybe Ryo is right. Perhaps I really am stupid." His voice is saturated in defeat. This upsets me but I want Yahei to succeed.

"Yahei, don't think so much. Listen to your intuition," I say. He sighs and plants his feet. "Now come at me!" I demand.

Yahei's new armor deem him a soldier but he is still my little brother. We now wear the same high collared bodysuit with long sleeves and heavy steel plates that guard our shoulders, elbows, and chest. He wears his hair long and up as Ryo does. I can see the insecurity beneath his cool gray eyes. Yahei never smiles anymore. His face is rigid like our father's now.

With rapid motions he is winding towards me, this time with more force. He goes over my head and lands behind me. Instead of striking he jumps, taking me by surprise. I put my sword up to block him. Once he's on the ground he swings for my legs. I dodge his attack before I charge and hit him in the chest with my shoulder, knocking him down. Yahei yelps in pain. I feel guilty but I'm trying my best to be a good teacher and brother. I pull him to his feet and dust him off.

"That was much better," I say. Yahei needs encouragement and I know Ryo is not one to offer such a luxury.

"Don't lie," he coughs.

"I'm not lying. You just need more practice," I say.

"What makes Ryo good at fighting?" asks Yahei.

"Ryo's only skill is using brute force. He has no other method," I spit.

"What about you, Riku?"

"I use my senses. I know what my opponent is going to do and counterstrike," I reply.

"How do you know though?"

"I just do. I know without knowing. You will learn," I assure him.

Yahei and I head back towards the castle. We run into Yama but she doesn't acknowledge us. None of us say a word.

Yama avoids eye contact with me. She keeps to herself but I know her and Rena are thick as thieves. They close their doors as I walk by. For all I know Yama is much crueler than Rena but not as vocal. She treats me as an unwanted guest. I can't recall the last time I heard Yama's voice, I couldn't pick it out in a crowd.

The white and red kimono she wears drags at her feet. Everywhere she goes her fragrant powdery jasmine perfume cloys the air. It's the same as our mother's scent. It permeates from her wavy white hair that lands above her shoulders. She snubs us with her sharp nose and adjusts her scarlet umbrella to block her view of us.

We march across the courtyard and our boots leave the insignia for the northern demon wolf clan in the snow. It's three mountain peaks with a sword. The emblem is meaningless now but centuries ago it was used to mark our territory.

The weapons we carry are also drenched in old traditions. They are crafted by the fire demons that dwell in the volcano. In between folding the layers of steel the blades are coated in clay from the fastest flowing river where the Mizuchi lives. It is rumored that this is what gives our swords an advantage. The Mizuchi is the water dragon. He is almost invisible, it's difficult to differentiate him from the waves in the water. They say the clay from the river is steeped in his demonic energy and it brings us luck.

"What will you do, big brother?" asks Yahei.

"I'm not sure."

"I don't want you to do something you'd regret," he says.

"What do you think I'll regret?"

"I think you'll regret letting Ryo be king, but you will regret taking on the position yourself even more." I'm impressed by Yahei's maturity.

"You are wise, little brother." I brush the snow from his hair.

"Riku?"

"What is it, Yahei?"

"I'm curious, why is it that you have such contempt towards the idea of leading?"

I stop walking and look at the symbols in the snow we've left behind. Yahei's footsteps next to mine seem out of place.

"I don't want that kind of power. Our people's way, our traditions and customs, they aren't mine," I answer.

"If our people's way is not our own, who do we belong to?" Yahei furrows his brows. I can tell he is torn between being the perfect soldier and son and listening to his own desires.

"We belong to ourselves," I assure him.

"Are you afraid of being alone?" he asks. I mull it over for a few moments before I speak.

"No, I'm not. I already feel alone in this hollow place. It would be better to just leave," I say, a bit too harsh. Yahei looks down as we near the castle. Then I hear his footsteps stop.

"Yahei, what are you doing?"

"We should go," he mumbles.

"What?"

"Me and you. We should leave here," he says, avoiding raising his voice. There are ears everywhere.

"No."

"Why not? You just said–" I cut him off.

"We're not talking about this anymore."

"You don't want me to go with you. Is that it?" Yahei's face is red and not from the cold.

"It's not that," I say.

"Then what? Tell me!" He demands.

I take him by the elbow and pull him away from the castle. I look into his eyes with bewilderment and he looks into mine. I lean in and scold him.

"Stop this nonsense," I say.

"Neither of us want to be here. Father wants you to fight him to the death and marry Hoshi. Is that the life you're going to choose, Riku? If that's what you want, I will respect your wishes. But you have to say it."

"We can't leave, Yahei. We just can't." I soften my tone and let go of his arm.

"Why?" His question is simple but one word holds numerous connotations. I can't begin to explain it to myself, let alone my brother.

"We just can't," I sigh. Yahei shoves me out of the way and I grind snowflakes in my teeth.

***

When Hoshi comes to visit I take her to places I know she likes, not the places where I go. Her favorite spot is by the lake. She's skipping stones at an impressive rate, clapping, and jumping as they reach the other side.

"Look, Riku! I did it again," she says.

Hoshi doesn't wear armor or go to war like me and my brothers and sister. She wears the white kimono signifying her role as a scholar and spiritual leader. Yama and Yuri wear the same thing. Yama presents herself as a clairvoyant in charge of teaching our people about the culture and history of wolf demons.

Yuri is her assistant. Every word of the demonic canon is analyzed and reanalyzed to make sure there is no misinterpretation. In our teachings there is the explanation of rules, the whats and the hows, but not the why. I throw a rock across the lake and it makes it halfway.

"Yeah, you're a lot better at this than me."

Hoshi isn't harsh or cruel. Most of the time we spend together she talks and I listen. If she wants me to pay attention to her she hangs on my neck and holds my shoulders. She's probably the only person who shows me affection. I could have loved her if I wasn't being forced to marry her.

I'm next in line for the crown and my marriage to her would unite the northern and western kingdoms. My army would be greater than any other's. After our wedding I'm to be the military commander for all seven clans. My job as king is to wage war. Yama is to step down and Hoshi will take over as head scholar and spiritual leader.

She picks up more snow and throws it at me in the playful way she does most things. Even though I'm not in love with her she still makes me smile. Besides my family, I don't socialize much. Hoshi keeps grabbing snow and tossing it at me.

"Hey, cut that out!" I joke.

"Make me," she laughs as she hits me in the face with another snowball. She begs me to chase her and takes off with amazing speed.

We race around the perimeter of the lake and everything's a white and green blur. Hoshi's kimono blends in but her sunlight hair stands out against the snow. We startle a herd of red deer and they join us in our race. I run past the largest buck and he makes eye contact with me. They have an unworldly stare. These are simple deer with no magic but white deer are sacred in the demon community.

Deep in the forest is a shrine of a half human half deer creature. It has been there for thousands of years. The white deer is a mystic, a messenger sent from the gods. I haven't seen one, or met anyone who spoke of the deer, but I believe she is out there. What message does she possess? Will she speak directly or is the message received telepathically?

Gods and demons. Ghosts and humans. What is left out of the books my sister and Hoshi read and teach from?

My father told me that in the beginning of time gods and demons roamed the earth together. At a certain point the gods retreated back to their spiritual plain but demons remained. I'm not paying attention when Hoshi ambushes me and we both fall into the snow.

"Hey, what was that for?"

"For being too slow," she says. Her eyes study me as I brush snow off my shoulder.

"You always beat me," I reply. I thought this would make her happy but she looks sad.

"I love you," she says.

"I love you, too." I help her to her feet and shake the snow out of her hair. It makes my chest tight when we speak this way. She's not a liar the way I am. To assuage my guilt I tell myself all the things I do love about her. I love her face, I love how light I feel in her presence, I love the way she looks when she's reading.

"Do you really?" she asks with concern.

"Don't be ridiculous," I answer and take her hand in mine.

I love her voice, I love when she does something silly and it makes me laugh, I love the way she loves me. We head towards the castle in silence. I suspect I've upset her. My family has been at my throat about the challenge. The challenge must happen before the wedding. I've been stalling and everyone can see through my excuses. My father says he can't keep lying but coming from the king that's a far cry. Even though I love him I break the cold warmonger's heart.

We pass two cranes with their beaks pointed to the sky. Their song is haunting as they call to one another. I can hear several more in the distance. They dance on long black legs and open their wings to the falling snow. They preen themselves, twisting their necks, and I make out red crowns on their heads. A chill moves through me and snowflakes stick in my eyelashes. I put my cloak around Hoshi's shoulders.

"Thank you," she whispers.

"Are you okay?" I ask.

"I sense something coming this way."

"We better hurry," I say and we glide on the wind. I open the castle door to be greeted by Ryo and Rena.

"Aren't you lovebirds sweet," Rena says in mock approval.

She's aware I've been putting off the challenge to delay the wedding. My sister is my sister and she knows me well.

"Father wants you in his study," Ryo spits at me. Hoshi tries to follow me but he puts his arm out. "Alone," he adds.

"Don't worry. We'll keep your fiance company," says Rena as she rubs Hoshi's shoulders in false sisterhood.

"Let's go over those wedding details. Shall we?" says Ryo. These two are relentless.

"How are we going to do your hair? Let's talk about your hair," chimes Rena as she takes Hoshi by the arm and runs her fingers through her sunny tresses.

I hate seeing my sister's filthy paws all over her. Knowing all the lives she's taken with them has corroded my trust.

"Close the door," barks my father as soon as I see him.

"What's the matter?"

"It's the boar demons. They are headed this way now. We were told that they have polluted the area with their demonic aura. Wretched beasts! They tear up the land and ruin the forest with their greed. They've had no food this winter and it has driven them to madness."

"When do we leave?"

"Tomorrow," he says.

***

In the early hours of dawn we raise our army. My father leads from the back, Yahei, Ryo, and Rena take the middle, and I'm in the front. Rena can't hide her excitement, she loves going into battle. Her war cry shakes the trees and the rodents inhabiting them flee. The king howls the loudest, then Yahei and Ryo join in. Our wolf brothers join us and run at our feet with obeisance. My family commands more of them and they come towards us from all directions. A white wolf with a strange mouth joins my side.

"Prepare yourself. Their starvation has led them further from themselves," he says.

"You have the gift of speech."

"I'm Satoru, demigod of the north."

"Thank you for your help," I say. It is rare to be assisted by a demigod, most of them disappeared with the gods.

"Anything for my brothers," he declares. A pang of shame pierces my heart. My disloyalty is an abomination in our world.

I signal for everyone to stop. The energy has shifted. The scent of wild boar lingers in the air and I hear the wet squeal of one of the demons. An enormous pig comes at me and I lock my sword with its tusks. Getting a better look at his eyes I see he is lost to his demonic power. Pus secretes from his wet snout. The eyes are no longer smooth, covered in bumps and clouded with hunger. The pupils are uneven. His mind numbed by his starvation.

"Stop this. We don't have to fight. Turn around now!" My words are met with nothing but cries from a wild animal.

"Leave! Don't make me kill you." He stops struggling for a moment, "Don't make me kill you," I repeat.

The boar demon's face is blank. I look over my shoulder to see Ryo and Rena foaming at the mouth, baring their canine teeth with wide grins. They are unhinged.

"Riku!" my father calls.

"I got this!" I assure him. "Leave," I whisper to the boar.

To my dismay he rears up and screams. The snow fallen ground rumbles as hundreds of hooves dig into the dirt. Without emotion I slide my blade through his skull. He falls over in a heap and black blood leaves a disgusting stench as it spills out.

My father calls us into formation and we enter the battlefield with our brothers. The wolves pack together to take them down. They hang from the boar demons' necks and nip at their ankles. I can hear hooves stomping and breaking bones. The cries of our brothers infuriates me but I can't let the rage consume me.

My father cut down several boar demons in one sweep of his sword. He is hostile, ruthless, and magnificent. His arms and chest heaving with strength. Pale skin pulled tight over his muscled body, worn but tough from centuries of war. His hair is pulled back tightly into a tail which waves in the roaring wind. Hearty grunts and growls roll through him as he attacks the enemy from every angle.

Ryo strikes them down with excessive force, putting his bare hands through the creature's chest, and ripping out its insides. He howls in laughter, licking his lips in satisfaction. The beast falls in a rumpled heap in the powdery snow. Liquid death leaks out from his stomach and mouth.

Rena runs through the open field and provokes every demon that she can. The wolves follow her every command. She bites and barks, baiting the boars into haphazardly fighting her and her small army. Wildly aggressive and never one to back down. Rena is a natural leader. Bold and resilient. She is a force to be reckoned with. If she took her other form we would all be dead.

Wolf demons can transform but everytime we do we lose a bit of our humanity. Rena has transformed so often she is on the verge of losing herself to the darkness. If this happens she won't be able to change back. She is forbidden from ever using her wolf form again. I avoid changing as much as possible and choose to fight as a man instead of using the beast.

Yahei is holding his own but struggling. The boar demons are sensing his hesitance and ganging up on him. I throw my sword through half a dozen of them. It hits the ground soaked in black blood that sizzles. The smell of it is repulsive and makes my eyes water, leaving ice in my lash line.

"Riku! Behind you!" shouts Yahei. I'm picking up my weapon when I look up to see a boar twice the size of the others. Using its dirty tusks it flings me into the trunk of a tree. The beast charges at me and I narrowly avoid being crushed by his massive hooves. It sweeps the tusks from side to side, kicking up snow, and roars at me. Charging again he grazes my left arm. Our blood is red, like human blood. I grab my wound and pull my hand away to observe the scarlet drops.

The air shifts and the ground vibrates beneath my feet. This time I'm ready for him. I turn around and embed my sword in between his glazed over eyes. Making my way to my little brother I see has creases in the corners of his eyes from squinting to block out the harsh winds. It's not snowing anymore but ground blizzards are just as fierce.

"Yahei, are you alright?" I ask.

"How did you do that?"

"Do what?"

"You knew exactly when the boar demon was behind you. If you struck any sooner or later you would have been dead," he says in a slow and serious voice.

"I told you, I know without knowing. You will learn," I tell him.

"You're hurt," he points out the cut. He rips off a piece of his obi and ties it around my arm.

"Thanks," I say. I'm appreciative of my little brother's kindness. It's a rarity in our family.

"Riku!" It's my father's voice.

The snow muffles the sounds of the battle but I know it's bad. The scent of blood, wolf and boar, saturates the air. I run in the direction of my father's voice and howl. He howls back and I follow the sound. The snow isn't even white anymore. It's a mix of ink and crimson. There are hundreds of paw prints next to the northern demon wolf insignia in the black slush.

"Riku!"

"What is it?" I shout over the storm.

"Transform," he orders.

"I can fight like this just fine," I protest. He is waving his arms in a wide motion. I can't see what he is talking about.

"My son, you must transform. Now!" he demands.

Battle is where I honor him but being ordered to change doesn't sit well with me. There's the howl of a dozen wolves and my father's face grows solemn. Through the haze of white and gray I notice what is causing all the commotion.

Down in the valley coming right at us is another army led by the biggest boar demon I've ever seen. He almost reaches the tops of the cedars. Behind me Ryo is losing his momentum. His strikes no longer have the vigor they did at the beginning of battle. Rena is sloppy and unable to hit her mark despite her prowess.

"Now, my son. You have to do it now!"

There is desperation in my father's tone this time. I hang my head and clench my fist. I don't want to do this but it is my duty to protect my family. It starts with my canine teeth, they grow sharp and my tongue bleeds. Moving to my shoulders and spine I feel my bones shatter and expand. The cracking of my sternum reverberates in my chest. The hair on the back of my neck stands up and I howl as my transformation is complete.

I have decent control of myself in this form unlike my brother and sister. As long as I don't let the rage consume me I'll be okay. The smaller boar demons drift in the snow as they approach me. Many of them turn around and run in the other direction. Their cowardice infuriates me but I keep my composure.

I roar into the face of the leader. He is smaller than I but still formidable. The great boar demon attempts to cut my throat with his filthy tusks. I go low and grab him by the ankle and knock him off his feet. The beast falls with a resounding thud shaking snow from the trees. The smaller creatures charge at me but they are easy to stomp and pick up with my jaws.

The leader rises and charges with his tusks towards my heart. I pivot and he misses but manages to hit me in the ribs. My bones are strong in this body and do not break. The impact stings but it doesn't hinder me. Here we are, enemy against enemy, walking circles around each other. I wait for him but he isn't charging like he was in the beginning. Occasionally he fakes a strike but I am aware of what he is thinking. I know his every move. He kicks up snow with his right hoof and screeches, spittle flying everywhere. It melts the snow where it lands. My growl is a grainy rumble in my throat. I don't talk to filthy pigs.

This time I make the move to attack. To my surprise he goes down without difficulty. Something is wrong. I take a few paces back and study the body of the boar. I didn't strike him hard enough to kill him. He uses my confusion against me and lunges. His tusks tear into the shoulder that was injured earlier. I yelp with anguish. Unable to control my hatred any longer I let go and succumb to the darkness. The last thing I remember is the sound of muscle shredding as I rip the boar demon's head off.

CHAPTER THREE

The Hollow Prince

I wake up in my room with an ache down my torso and my left shoulder throbbing. Lifting away the blanket, I see my right side is bruised from my chest to my hip. Purple and green contusions decorate my ribs. My shoulder is worse. It's covered in thick bandages, but I can see the spots where blood has been seeping out. I try to sit up but it sends a shooting pain through my body and I choose to lie down instead. Staring up at the ceiling, I piece together what happened after my transformation. I was myself, I was in control, but then the pig enraged me. There's a knock at my door.

"Come in," I say. It's my little sister.

"Are you okay, Riku?" She looks at me with her sad and tired eyes.

"I'm fine, Yuri. Don't worry," I say and reach for her hand.

"Do you remember what happened?" Yuri's voice is mousy. Rena hates it and makes fun of her all the time. I'd love to rip out Rena's vocal cords.

"A little bit." I close my eyes and focus on the coolness of her hand.

"Father said you were spectacular."

"Did he?" I open one eye at her.

"Yes, he is very proud."

"Good," I say. She sits quietly but I can sense she wants to say more. "What is it?" I ask her.

"It's just...nevermind."

"I'm your big brother, tell me."

"How can you be like father and Ryo? They have soot where their hearts should be. It's hard to imagine you killing a whole army of boar demons and their leader by yourself," she says. I didn't realize I took them all on by myself.

"Hey, listen. I'm nothing like them," I protest.

"You are but you aren't!" She pulls her hands from mine and bunches them into two tiny fists.

"What's wrong? Why are you mad at me? I thought we were on the same side."

"I'm not mad at you. I'm mad at our culture. I hate all the violence, the war mongering, and the excessive wealth. We live up on the mountain with more food than we could ever eat while people die in the villages below from famine. How can we be so high and mighty above the weak and suffering? What gives us the right?" she shouts. This is unusual, Yuri never has outbursts or raises her voice to me.

"I'm tired of our culture, too. It doesn't suit us. We still have a soul," I tell her.

"How can you stand being Father's puppet for glory?"

"I am trying to take it one day at a time. How do you stand being Yama's underling?" I ask.

"I can't! She makes me read from the demonic canon. Rubbish that is drenched in old principals that are improper. Then we spread it to the others in the form of spiritual enlightenment."

"I know, Yuri. It hurts me to see you live like this."

"Me? What about you! Look at you!" she shrieks and pulls the blanket away from my shoulder.

As if to prove her point, another spray of blood begins to seep through the bandage. I stare into the cold gray eyes of my sister and see a fire burning inside.

"Did something happen?" I ask. She hangs her head and looks away as she speaks.

"Rena caught me giving a boy in the village radishes. She scolded me for consorting with humans like a sheep. But they are starving, Riku!"

"You know we're not supposed to leave the mountains," I start.

"I know one day you will leave us for good, so don't tell me where I can and can't go."

"That's not true."

"Don't lie to me, big brother. Our hearts are the same," she says as she gets up to leave.

"Yuri, wait!" I shout but she closes the door on me.

The pain moves through my spine as I sit up. My little sister surprises me. Perhaps she is not the timid person I knew her to be. Even in all my disobedience I have never left the mountains. Yuri went all the way to the bottom and met a human boy. She gave him food from our crops. I smile to myself, my sister and I are the same in different ways. There's another knock at the door.

"Come in," I say expecting Yuri. I'm disappointed to see Rena holding a tray of food.

"Hello, little brother." She smiles her wicked grin at me.

Her dark lips wash out her fair skin and the arch of her eyebrows makes her look like a demented spirit.

"What do you want, Rena?" I moan and pull the blanket over my face. She rips it off me and throws it across the room. Somehow she can throw something soft and it hits the ground as hard as possible.

"What? Can't your big sister bring you some nourishing food after slaying an army by yourself," she says in her pretentious voice. Rena sets down the tray and shoves a skewered fish at me. "You need to eat, regain your strength." I'm sure she is going to stick it down my throat so I grab it from her and take a bite.

"There, you happy now?"

"Yes, very. I'm so proud of you," she says. It's subtle but I know she's being genuine. I'm not hungry but I keep eating so I don't have to talk to her.

"You were magnificent. I never gave you enough credit in the past but I have to hand it to you, Riku. You are a truly beautiful killer."

"I'm not a killer," I spit.

"Oh, no? What would you call me if I decimated an army by myself?" she hisses at me. Her silver eyes are sly and suspicious. It's hard to keep eye contact but I refuse to back down.

"We are Father's puppets, nothing more," I say.

In one swift motion she picks up a bowl from the tray and throws it into the wall. Loud shattering as a hundred pieces hit the floor but she doesn't look at the mess or turn to the sound, her eyes remain locked on me.

"We are glorious. Majestic beasts, unique from the demons who lack speech like the boar. We are above the insects, rodents, and fish. Why do you squander what has been given to you, little brother?"

"I can't squander something I don't believe in," I answer. Her fists beg to choke me out.

"Tell me, what is it you believe in?" she asks.

"I don't believe in anything."

"The King is God. God is everything," she recites from the ancient books, "Nothing without you," she says as she touches two fingers to her lips before pointing at me.

"What is a king or a god without followers? Only an idea. You live in a fantasy," I growl at her.

"What is a nonbeliever? Just an outsider," she says. Her silky hair slides across her back as she slips out the door.

***

Due to my injuries I'm allowed to skip my daily chores. No fighting lessons, no teachings, or war strategies. Only Matsu, our servant, and I are in the castle right now. Matsu is of short stature but this does not limit his abilities. My father chose him for his proficiency. Lucky for me Matsu takes his job seriously and does not attempt to be too friendly or nosy.

"Master Riku, how are you faring today?"

"I'm fine. And just call me Riku."

"Master Riku, would you like some tea?" he asks, ignoring me on purpose.

"Yes, thank you."

"I'll bring it to you in your room. Your father wants you to rest." Matsu is my father's voice. He gives me orders even when he's not around.

"Of course," I reply.

I sit by the window and look down at the rivers and lake below. There is a village to the east with smoke rising from the miniscule homes. That must be where Yuri met the human boy. Her generosity impresses me. I've been selfish, only thinking of myself. I don't understand the human world but I'm intrigued by it. My little sister knows their suffering. I'm curious about the depths of their pain. Father says their lives carry no more importance than the life of an ant. I hear rapping at the door.

"Come in," I say. To my dismay it's not Matsu, it's Ryo.

"Riku, my dear boy. I brought your tea," he announces.

"Thanks," I reply.

He hands the cup to me but I refuse to drink anything my older brother gives me. I set it down. Ryo is the tallest in our family. I don't crane my neck to look up at him and continue staring out the window.

"Have you heard about Yuri's infatuation with the human boy?" he asks with contempt.

"I have," my voice is flat as I speak.

"You two might be strays but Yahei is ours."

"I'm not a stray," I say, trying to hide my impatience.

"Not yet, little brother."

"I'm damned if I stay, I'm damned if I go." Ryo's fingers are digging into my face. His eyes are my eyes glaring back at me.

"Look at you, you pathetic whelp. How can I honor you if you don't even honor yourself? Father's sight must be broken because I can't see what he admires in you."

"I've tried to convince Father to challenge you instead. He sees that you are lacking what it takes to be king," I say. Ryo's fingers dig in deeper.

"Father is blind to the truth!" shouts Ryo.

"What truth? Everything on the mountain is a lie." My brother lets go of my face and I feel blood dripping below my eye where he scratched me.

"Then go live down there with the humans. I'm sure they would gladly accept a stray dog like you," Ryo laughs.

"Why can't we help them?" I ask without thinking. Ryo's jaw drops and he slams his fist into the wall.

"Help them? Why would we help them? They are vermin! They violate the forest and each other. We live in different worlds. Their laws are not our laws," he spits.

"Have you ever talked to one of them?"

"I don't need to. Believe it or not little brother, but I've witnessed plenty in my six-hundred years. Stop wondering about them. You'll end up hopeless and in love like our baby sister," Ryo growls in his arrogant tone.

"I have Hoshi," I say. His body shakes with laughter.

"The only one you've convinced is Hoshi. Which is a shame, she is such a nice girl. Too nice for you, runt. She really should be my wife," he says. My hand is around his neck. I squeeze it as I bring us face to face.

"Don't talk about her. Don't you ever talk about her. I never want to hear her name come out of your mouth again," I say and we are both shocked by my protectiveness.

Maybe I don't love Hoshi the way I'm supposed to but hearing my brother say vile things about her makes the blood rot in my veins. He's right. She's too good for me. She's also too good for him. I wish she had better options. Neither of us is worthy.

"He has an ounce of honor in him after all," Ryo sings as he exits my room.

After I can no longer hear his footsteps I pour the drink he gave me out the window. There's another knock at the door and I'm ready to throw the teacup at Ryo.

"What do you want?" I shout. To my surprise it's Yama this time. I can't recall the last time we spoke. She glides across the wooden floor with her kimono dragging behind her, "Sorry. Why are you here, Yama?" I ask.

She has amber eyes like me and Father but hers are intelligent and inquisitive, unlike Ryo's. Standing next to me I smell her sticky sweet jasmine perfume that reminds me of our mother. Lifting up my chin she looks into my eyes, studying me as though I am sacred script.

"Yes, I see it now."

"See what?"

"Why Father wants you to lead," she speaks in riddles.

It's from the constant combing over of the demonic canon. Her red mouth is glossy and thin. It stands out like blood on fresh snow. My sister has black eyelashes that remind me of butterfly legs.

"What do you see?"

"Someone with great power and an interesting fate."

"Interesting? Have you ever been interested in what happens to me?"

"Yes. I had a vision of you."

"A vision?"

"You were guided by the white deer. There was fire everywhere. Carrying something precious in your arms as you walked on sacred grounds," she says in her professorial voice.

This is bizarre. My sister Yama hardly gives me the time of day but now she is speaking of prophecies and premonitions.

"Does that mean I'm not meant to be king?"

"Perhaps. What if you are destined for something else? Something more. The white deer is revered. I would follow the gods' messenger before abiding by our father's wishes," she says as she sits next to me.

I've never heard my older siblings speak about our father with such defiance. Feeling uneasy I get up to pace around the room.

"What are you saying?" I ask.

"I'm telling you the truth. I know our ways are strict. It can be difficult to understand. I think more is being asked of you than to become a military leader."

"You think I should refuse the challenge?"

"I can't decide that for you. All I know is what I saw. You and the white deer running through fire. It's important, Riku."

Could my sister be right? How can I trust someone I don't know? This could be a trick. I'm curious though, what does the vision mean?

"I have a lot to think about," I say, wanting to be alone. Understanding my meaning she gets up to leave and as she exits she puts her hand on my chest.

"Ryo's loyalty to Father is dangerous. Be wary, little brother." She is gone without a sound and I am left with my thoughts that pull me in a hundred different directions.

***

"Nothing without you," says my father as he touches two fingers to his lips before pointing at me. I do the same.

"Nothing without you," I mimic.

"Today is the day," he declares. The challenge is unavoidable. I've put it off too long.

"Father, please reconsider."

"No, my son. I choose you," he says.

I want to protest more but he moves past me and out of the castle. I detached from the idea of killing my father years ago and now I feel the dread course through my veins like tar. My heart is heavy but the crown weighs more.

Our people gather around the arena where the challenges take place. The servants are hard at work crafting a feast for the reception. The smells blend together and all of a sudden I'm sick to my stomach. Running outside I find a secluded place around the castle and vomit. I've had my shoulders dislocated, ribs splintered, and my nose broken but nothing compared to this. For the most part I have treated this day as a joke. Now it's here and I'm ill prepared.

I rest my hands on my knees and put my head down. Dammit, there has to be another way. Remembering what Yama said about the white deer makes me wonder if I have a choice. This life has never felt right to me. I don't allow myself to hope or dream but today I ache for the glimmer of salvation. Daring to break from the pack is a disgrace. I have always protected my family. Even if it meant sacrificing pieces of myself. For my father I have killed, stolen, and destroyed. Today he asks me to take his life. Loving him hasn't been easy but I love him still. Why is our culture cruel enough to request his death?

"Riku?" Yahei is standing behind me. Feeling ashamed I wipe the vomit from my mouth and straighten up.

"Yes?" I cough.

"I'm worried," he says.

"About what?"

"About what will become of our family. What will become of you?"

"I don't know, Yahei. I wish I did."

"We all know what will happen if Ryo leads," he delivers his statement with annoyance.

"What do you mean?" I ask.

"If you don't resume the throne we are all doomed to another thousand years of war and excess."

"There is nothing we can do to stop it. I will be forced to do what our father has done," I snap.

"The King is God. God is everything. You could do whatever you want and who would stop you? Everyone is brainwashed into witnessing the alpha as divine. You could change us!" he shouts.

"You know as well as I that Rena and Ryo will never let that happen."

"Yuri told me of Yama's vision. Even she isn't so dense as to believe everything must happen literally," he informs me.

"Since when do you trust Yama?"

"I don't. But she takes her job seriously. I believe she has had the realization that a book is just a book." My brother's face is made of stone.

"I'm not sure what to do," I confess.

"Please, Riku. Take the crown. Our people won't know peace under Ryo's command."

"I'll try," I say.

"Promise then. Promise you will try," he demands.

"I promise." I don't know if I'm lying or not.

The sound of drums rumbles in the distance. The challenge will begin soon. I go back inside and clean my face and my teeth. I stare at myself in the mirror and wonder if this is who I am. What am I to the white deer?

The drums get louder as the sun lowers in the sky. The challenge can happen anytime of year but always at sunset. As I walk to the arena in a disconnected daze our people cheer for me. They bow to me and throw rice and flowers at my feet. Everyone is in high spirits as I am pulled towards the place of my fate.

Men hold out their hands palm up and wait for me to place my hand above theirs. The people make a path for me but all the invasive touching makes me feel like I'm not moving. Rice crunches under my boots. It's louder than the unanimous voices of the wolf demons. I know they scream my name in honor but I drown it out, grain by grain.

Somehow I make it past the enormous crowd and enter the arena. My father bows to me and the cheering ceases. I bow back in response as the tradition instructs. He puts two fingers to his lips and recites from the canon, "Nothing without you."

"Nothing without you," I imitate.

He draws his sword and I draw mine. The challenge has begun. We lock eyes and I look into my father's soul. His moves are difficult to predict because he often changes his strategy at the last moment. I know my father, his cleverness is my cleverness. Making a move to strike first he blocks me, as I knew he would. The old man's face is emotionless. He aims for my legs but I jump and kick him into the ground. The snow is thin. Winter is almost over.

Recovering quickly he swings the sword at my chest leaving a faint scratch in the armor. My name is in a thousand different mouths. I can't concentrate. To convince my father of my compliance I at least have to put on a good show. Maybe it would be better to die as I am rather than live on as the king. Foolish of me to think I could escape this situation.

We spar with impressive skill as the sun sets on the horizon turning the sky blossom pink and indigo. My father notices I'm not fighting with the ferocity necessary. He starts coming at me with more intensity. Persistent blows leave me little room to fight back. I understand he is trying to provoke me but I don't take the bait.

Gasps and shouting surround the arena. I spot my older brother and sister in the crowd. They cross their arms and watch me and our father battle with smug expressions. I promised Yahei I would try to win but I don't know what I will do either way. To please the crowd I fling my father off of me and bring my blade down. Blood oozes from a nasty gash in his left arm. The cries of our people erupt into a chant.

"Nothing without you," they say. My father rises and throws a punch into my right temple. It stings and blurs my vision.

"Nothing without you," repeat the voices. He comes at me and without any plan of how to end this I block him.

"Do it," he growls at me.

I increase the pressure hoping the tension would give me time to think. Observing the crowd behind him I see Yuri, her hands are clasped at her chest. Our last conversation she said I was nothing like our father.

I stare into his eyes, amber and cold, and make a decision I may regret. Using the tension to my advantage I pull away and dodge his immediate attack. Before he can resume brutalizing me I jump over the arena wall and take off down the mountain.

CHAPTER FOUR

No One

Slinking through the forest all night leads me to the village. I couldn't sleep. What have I done? After my weak escape my father had to choose another. It will be Ryo, I just know it. The kingdom won't be forgiving of my absence. I don't know why I'm here. For the entirety of my journey I've been lost in my head. How did Yuri have the courage to come out this far on her own? It's sunny but a chill hangs in the air. I have never seen humans up close. On occasion we have spied them on our journeys but we do not disturb them and they do not disturb us.

Standing at the treeline I watch with fascination at the simpleness of their lives. Mothers lift their young and hold their hands as they carry out their day. There are men working on various projects throughout the village. They chop wood, fold steel, and transport various goods using horses. Besides the mothers and their children there are women washing clothes in icy water. Their faces are thin and their wrists are frail. Yuri was right, it's obvious they don't have enough food. Children cough from illness and spit yellow mucus. To the south are multiple fields but they are barren. There is only dirt where there should be turnips and cabbages. The rice paddies are flooded and the ground is damaged.

In all my life I've never witnessed abject poverty. Reminded of the extreme wealth I come from I scorn my ungratefulness. I am engrossed by the happenings of humans but the scent of a demon raises the hair on the back of my neck. This isn't a wolf. With great stealth I make my way through the foliage. I walk with caution, careful not to announce my presence.

"Don't worry. I'll bring her back when I'm done," says a sonorous voice.

"Please. Please, don't hurt her."

"I gave you what you wanted. I've come to collect," he laughs.

Taking cover in the shadow of the trees I sneak closer to see who the voices belong to. A demon with long black hair wearing the fur of a bear holds a young woman in his arms. He wears red trousers and expensive boots. His broad chest is bare. Dark olive skin shifts over the muscles. The young woman squirms under his grasp but he doesn't let go.

"Please, don't do this. We can give you something else," begs a man. He's on his knees. This must be the woman's husband.

"Really? What else do you have that is of value to me?" hisses the demon through sharp fangs. The man hangs his head and weeps.

"It's okay. Everything is going to be okay," says the woman attempting to comfort him. As she reaches for her husband's hand the demon pulls her away and she shrieks.

"You should be appreciative of my generosity. One day I'll take one of the women and I'll never bring her back. Rest easy knowing at least your love will return," says the demon in the bear fur. He wears the head as a hood that covers his face.

With that he drags the young woman by the wrist and leads her into the forest. She looks over her shoulder at her husband who remains on his knees with tears streaming down his face. He holds out his hand and grabs the air. I see her mouth the words "I love you" as she vanishes into the dark woods. The man is hysterical. Feeling the rage build up in me I am tempted to confront the demon. I don't know how to help. It isn't any of my business but I can't contain my curiosity. I exit the treeline and stand in front of the man. He trembles from fright and smells of tobacco and salt.

"If you are here to kill me then do it now," he says.

"Why would I kill you?" I ask.

"You are not one of Kasai's cohorts?"

"Who is Kasai?"

"He is the fire demon who took my wife. We have been starving all winter. In our desperation my wife agreed to be Kasai's for one night in exchange for some measly rice," he says before continuing to sob. On impulse I think of killing Kasai. The image is vivid and shakes me to my core.

"Perhaps I can be of assistance," I say and draw my sword to demonstrate.

"You are noble and kind. I can see it in your eyes. Unfortunately you can't help me. You can't help any of us who have lost our wife or sister to Kasai. Sure, they come back after a day, maybe a week. But they return as ruined shells of who they used to be," says the man as he bows to me.

"What if I strike him down? Then he won't be able to hurt the women anymore," I say.

"Kasai is no ordinary demon. He is from The Underworld. Making a deal with him is absolute. We can not rescind our promises to him," he informs me.

"I'm sorry. I wish I could help you," I offer.

"Thank you, noble demon. Please, tell me your name."

"My name is Riku."

***

It's late in the day as I arrive back at the castle. The cheers and the bloodlust from yesterday echo in my head. I feel their hands all over me and it sends a shiver through my body. No one is in the courtyard or garden. The house is eerie, the fire isn't lit, and neither are the lanterns.

"Hello?" I call to the empty room.

No reply. Creeping through the dark halls I hear a soft cry. It's coming from Yuri's room. I knock on her door and let myself in. To my horror my sister is covered in blood, it's splattered across her white kimono, and face.

"Yuri! Are you okay?" I rush to my sister's side.

"It's not my blood," she sobs.

"It's Father's, isn't it?"

"Yes," she says but I already knew the answer. I sigh with relief but notice her eyebrows are furrowed causing deep creases in her forehead, "Ryo is king now," she adds.

"What happened?" I ask.

"What we all knew would happen but it was terrible, Riku."

"We have been preparing for this our whole lives," I say.

"You don't understand." Her voice is strained. She buries her face in her hands and I can't hear her through her muffled cries. Attempting to comfort my sister I put my arm around her.

"It's okay, Yuri. It'll be okay."

"No, it's not! Ryo is a monster! Father bled out in the mud like a butchered pig. The challenge was over but Ryo wasn't satisfied. I was right there when he cut off Father's head!" she shouts.

My eyes are wide with surprise. Ryo is merciless but even I am shocked at his disrespect towards our father. How could a loyal son be capable of something so foul?

"I went to the human village," I announce and she stops sobbing.

"You did?"

"I saw the starvation and poverty. Even worse, I saw a demon preying upon the women of the village. Giving themselves to him for a meager supply of food."

"I can't turn a blind eye," she whispers.

"What do you mean?"

"If we do not witness any suffering but our own, how can we know who we truly are?" I am amazed by my sister's deep proclamation.

"I wish I knew the answer," I say and get up to leave but Yuri grabs my sleeve.

"The kingdom holds you in contempt. Watch your back," she says.

I nod and slip out the door. Feeling my breathing constrict I step outside for some air to fight the nausea. Yellow and purple petals wither in the snow. The grains of rice caked in mud bring up a new wave of shame. People starve below while we throw food into the dirt to appease our traditions.

"There you are," says Ryo as he rounds the corner.

"Back off!" I snap at him.

"Never," he mutters as he elbows me in the mouth. My saliva tastes metallic as it mixes with blood. I spit it in his face.

"You dare demean the king, little brother?" he asks, smearing the red liquid across his cheek with the back of his hand.

"You'll never be half the king our father was."

"This is fitting. First you defy him and now you defend him."

"You hold him in the highest regard, then take off his head. How could you, Ryo?"

"I do what I have to," he growls, "Nothing without you, little brother."

"I won't," I snarl.

"What did you just say, you worthless whelp?"

"I won't say it. Especially under your rule."

"You should have killed Father when you had the chance," he says and aims for my throat.

I duck before tossing him away from me. The last of the snow catches his fall. Ryo attacks me again but I can fight him easily knowing his only tactic is to use brute force.

"Why, Ryo? We don't have to fight," I say through clenched teeth.

"Yes, we do. Nothing without you," he repeats. I refuse to say it back. "Filthy stray," he hurls the words at me with a jagged edge.

"A stray, a runt, a brother, who am I to you?" I ask.

"No one," his words slice through me.

The anger boils over and I can't contain my rage any longer. My eyes burn red with demonic hatred. I rush my brother with everything I have. He laughs as I strike him down and step on his chest. I aim the sword at his heart. Even as I lose myself to the darkness I sense something is off. My sister Yama's voice is a whisper in my ear, "Ryo's loyalty to Father is dangerous. Be wary, little brother."

"Do it, Riku. Tear out my heart. Mother would be so proud," his voice is lilting and strange.

At that moment I realized what he was trying to do. He wants me to kill him. Even in death my father has a hold on us all. Ryo's need to obey him is stronger than his thirst for power. I am nothing like my family. They would die to win. I was born to lose. I remove my boot from his chest.

"The King is God. God is everything," he chokes.

I give him a hard kick to the ribs and he yelps. I hide in my room for the rest of the night. Matsu checks on me but I tell him to leave me be. Pulling the blanket over myself I put my hand to my temple where my father struck me. That was the last time he touched me. I will never see him again. Disappearing inside myself I wonder if the gods cry, too.

***

Three days of sulking in my room has left me restless. No one has knocked on my door besides Matsu. I'm anxious to see what Ryo has in store for us. Under his rule we will be at war more often than not. It gives me a headache between the eyes. I think about my father and how he governed our people. Before I would call him nothing but a warmonger. Now I see that he was formidable, strategic, and intuitive. Ryo will never be able to live up to his standards. From my bed I stare out the window and pray for redemption. Someone is entering my room but I don't bother to look up.

"Here, you need to take care of yourself." It's Yama.

She holds a tray of food out to me. My sister has never brought me anything and I turn my nose up at it. Giving me a pious look she picks up a strawberry and eats it.

"It's not poison."

"Leave me alone," I mumble as I turn to my side.

"You've always been stubborn but come on, eat something. Please," she says.

"Why are you being so nice to me? I thought you hated me," I bark at her.

Yama is laughing behind me. She laughs the way I imagine the gods would. I look over my shoulder to see her red mouth stretched across her face.

"Hate you? You are my brother, Riku. I could never hate you." Her answer is sincere.

"You and I haven't spoken in years. What is it you want? You are curious about the white deer but I don't know anything about that."

"I must apologize. Being a spiritual leader isn't easy. But neither is being asked to murder for prestige," she says.

"Don't you skim over that book a hundred times a day? I thought it was the word of the almighty."

"I have been forced to read from the sacred scripts all my life. For many years I thought I was doing my duty. After my vision of you and the white deer something became apparent."

"What is that?"

"That you are different. You are meant for more."

"If only I knew what that was," I sigh. My sister sits across from me and motions to the tray of food. I pick up an apple and take a bite.

"Riku, I need to tell you something."

"What?"

"I've been jealous of you. The way you are able to listen to your heart. You may have disobeyed our father at times but he knew you loved him. I wish I was able to have the strength you have," her voice is a whisper. Yama's confession catches me off guard. Her hand is cool silk on my face. "You must live for you now," she says.

"Yama, wait!"

"Yes?" she asks.

"In the vision you said I was carrying something precious. What was it?"

"I'm not sure. Once you have it, guard it with your life. I'm sorry, I wish I could tell you more." She's gone without a sound.

I wash my face and run my fingers through my disheveled hair. The bruise on the right side of my face has healed. Feeling the need to walk around I get dressed and exit my room. The castle has a sepulchral atmosphere. Our house is extravagant but uninviting. At first I think no one is home but then I hear voices at the end of the corridor. The wooden floor creaks beneath my boots as I make my way towards the sound.

"He has finally decided to join us," Ryo sings through his teeth. Hoshi is at his side.

"Hoshi–" I trail off. I don't know what to say.

"Are you here to congratulate us?" he taunts.

"You can't be serious!" I shout.

"Hold your temper, little brother. You didn't think she'd still marry you, did you?" He puts his arms around Hoshi and she doesn't reject his advance.

"Really, Hoshi? You're going to marry Ryo?" I ask. I don't mean to but I raise my voice and she starts to cry.

"I waited for you! All these years I've waited for you!" she screams at me.

"I'm sorry–"

"No, you're not! You might say you're sorry and act like you're remorseful but you aren't. I loved you Riku. How could you betray me?"

Ryo tightens his grip around her. I remember him putting his hand through the boar demon and shredding it apart. Now that hand is on her shoulder. Instead of pulling away she embraces him.

"I thought you were better than this, Hoshi," I say and dart out of the castle.

Knowing my brother's hand was roaming her body disgusts me. I am a fool, I didn't even think about Hoshi when I fled from the challenge. How could I be so selfish? She should refuse him but now I know the depths of her faith. We could never be together. Everyone tells me what I am. They call me privileged, honored, and blessed. To me these things are a curse. Bad luck charms that bring nothing but tragedy.

CHAPTER FIVE

The White Deer

Yuri and I are in the garden. Plum blossoms are starting to open. They symbolize renewal. My little sister has stopped crying but she has dark circles under her eyes. I watch her admire the purple and gold flowers. This has been most difficult for her. I was our father's favorite but she was his baby girl. He always came back from war with presents for her, gold jewelry and silk. My father could fight an army by himself. I wince at the thought of Ryo taking off his head. Smoke rises from the houses down in the valley. Yuri catches me looking at them.

"How do they make you feel?" she asks.

"I'm not sure."

"Rena and Ryo threatened to kill the human boy I gave food to," she admits.

"I won't let them do that," I assure her.

"They make me feel strong. I want to protect them. I love him, Riku." My sister's sadness is my sadness.

"I offered to kill the demon that is terrorizing the village. I feel the urge to protect them as well," I say. Before we can speak any further on the matter my sister Rena is breathing down our necks.

"Little brother," she pinches my ear and I yelp.

"Leave us alone," says Yuri.

"Baby sister," Rena coos as she reaches for Yuri's face but I grab her wrist.

"Don't," I snap.

"What? Can't I show some affection to my dear baby sister?" Rena growls at me.

"Go away," groans Yuri.

"You'll thank me someday," says Rena as she pulls away from my grip. I could crush every bone in her arm.

"Leave her be!" I shout.

Rena bares her canines at me but says nothing. As I turn to comfort Yuri I feel her tackle me. She sits on my chest and punches me in the face several times.

"You could have been king. You could have had everything! How could you give it all up?" she asks with our noses touching.

"Ryo is king now, shouldn't that please you?"

"Ryo is an imbecile. Don't toy with me, little brother."

I laugh at this and spray blood all over Rena. Scarlet liquid freckles her pale skin. Not a muscle twitches beneath her cool facade. She doesn't even blink.

"It's too late now," I say.

"Soon Hoshi and Ryo will be married and expecting a child. How does that sit with you?"

"Hoshi was never mine."

"I don't understand it. How can you resist all that power, Riku?" She narrows her weaponized steel colored eyes at me.

"Get off of him!" cries Yuri. Rena glares at her but then notices the village in the distance.

"Is that it? Your precious humanity? You two really are pathetic," she says as she gets up and stares at the smoke rising from the valley.

***

Yahei hasn't spoken to me since the day of the challenge. I suspect he's angry with me for breaking my promise. In his eyes I failed him. Interestingly enough it is Yama who seeks me out most days. The lake is no longer frozen over. Its water is tranquil and blue green like the obi we wear. I'm staring at my reflection in the water and Yama appears next to me. She moves like a ghost. I have to make sure she leaves footprints.

"What are you doing, little brother?" she asks.

"Thinking," I answer.

The sun is high in the sky casting an ethereal glow on the lake. This was Hoshi's favorite place to go. I thought I'd miss her more but after witnessing her embrace Ryo I no longer wish to see her. I'm pulled from my thoughts as Yama wades into the water.

"Come, I will show you your destiny," she says.

The water is to her waist. She motions for me to join her in the lake. Yama is enigmatic, I have never known what she is thinking. I step into the blue green and kick up silt from the bottom on my way to her. She places one hand on my chest and the other behind my neck.

"Do you trust me, Riku?" she asks. I don't know if I do.

"Yes," I say.

Without any hesitation Yama shoves my head under the water. She is going to drown me! I thrash in her arms but to my astonishment my sister is quite strong. Bubbles escape from my mouth as I fight her. I can see her red lips and wavy white hair through the surface of the water. Of all the siblings I thought would murder me I did not expect it to be Yama.

The smell of smoke is heavy in the air. It's tinged with a rotten odor. I'm running as fast as I can. To my left I catch a glimpse of white in the ink black darkness. The sacred deer! I follow it through the forest. It takes me to a village that's burning to the ground. The deer stares at me. I think it wants me to go in. Stepping through the broken structures I notice bodies ripped apart. Their blood soaks into the dirt staining it purple. In my arms is something wrapped in my cloak. I can't see what it is but I know it's important.

"Are you alright?" Yama's voice is concerned and motherly.

I choke on the air and cough up the water in my lungs. I'm about to scold her but see that she is smiling.

"What are you doing, Yama? Are you trying to kill me, too?"

"Did you see it?"

"Yes, I saw the white deer." I cough. Yama gives me a thoughtful nod.

"Keep your eyes open for her. She has a message for you."

"I still don't know what the vision means."

"You don't have to know what it means. Just remember it, okay?"

she says and guides me out of the lake.

***

It's the day of Ryo and Hoshi's wedding. I don't attend and hide in my room instead. The decadence of the celebration vexes me. This would have been my wedding. Looking out the window I see everyone dancing at the reception. Giant bouquets of flowers sit in gold urns that line the path. There's too many types of food and the pungent scent tempts me to empty the contents of my stomach. I get back in bed and pull the blanket over myself.

I don't mean to but I fall asleep. I sleep away most of the days. Even if I'm not tired I force myself to sleep. It's the closest thing to being dead. As I look out the window I see that it is night. The moon is full and I hear our people howl at it. Their song is ringing in my ears. I cover my face with my pillow.

I can't breathe. I try to get up but feel four hands on me, two holding my legs and another pair smothering me with the pillow. My hands are under theirs and they use my body against me. I flail my torso and manage to kick whoever has my legs off me. Pressing my back into the floor I slide my body out from underneath my attackers. I look up to see Yahei's stony face. Ryo holds the pillow he tried to suffocate me with.

"I would expect this from Rena, but not you Yahei."

"You broke your promise," his tone is cold.

"I did try–" I start.

"Not hard enough!" he growls and lunges at me, pinning me against the wall.

"I'm sorry," I say.

"You're sorry an awful lot, big brother."

"Why are you doing this?"

"We are doing what we have to do. Your disloyalty is a disgrace. It should be met with severe punishment," says Ryo. He stands behind Yahei and eggs him on.

"You have the crown, you have Hoshi, you have everything now. Isn't that what you wanted?" I ask.

"It was supposed to be you, Riku. Why did you run away? You

traitor!" shouts Yahei. Ryo puts his hand on his shoulder.

"The challenge was turned into a scandal. Our people's faith is shaken," says Ryo.

"The challenge is a scandal because you cut off his head! You're the traitor," I bark.

"Shut up, runt!" screams Ryo. Yahei increases the pressure on my neck.

"Please, Yahei. This isn't you."

"This is who I am now," he says in a flat tone that matches his face.

My heart breaks as my little brother digs in with his elbow. Ever since I can remember Rena and Ryo have brutalized me. I thought Yama hated me too but in the days since the challenge she has shown me the most kindness.

I can handle Ryo and Rena's abuse but not my little brother's. The day he suggested we both leave this place comes to mind. He didn't want this life but now under Ryo's rule he is brainwashed into executing me.

"Look, Yahei. You're making him cry. Are you sad, little brother? Is our baby brother breaking that foolish heart of yours?" taunts Ryo.

I headbutt Yahei and he falls down in an instant. Then I pounce on Ryo and bash his head into the floor.

"Why can't you just leave me be, Ryo?"

"The blame is on you," he chokes.

I look over at Yahei. His face is slack and the stony expression is gone as he lay unconscious. I smack Ryo's head into the floor until blood seeps out of his ears.

"I'm leaving," I snarl.

"If you leave the mountain, you can never come back."

"I'm never coming back." I step away from Ryo and grab my armor and my sword.

"Not even for Hoshi? I'm sure she'll call your name when I have her tonight," he laughs.

I ball up my fist and resist the urge to murder my brother. I know that's what he wants. Even now he wants me to be king. I stand over him and dig my fingers into his face.

"If I find out you hurt her in any way I'll come back just to make you wish you were dead," I say. I'm running through the courtyard when I hear Yuri beside me.

"Riku, where are you going?"

"I can't stay here."

"Please! Please, don't leave me here with them," she begs.

"I have to go, Yuri. I'm sorry."

"Take me with you!" she cries and grabs my hand.

"I can't."

"Why?"

"Because I don't even know what I'm doing. I don't know anything about the outside world. I can't protect you out there!" I shout in frustration.

"How is leaving me here any better than what's beyond the mountains?"

Her face is streaked with tears. I kneel down and look my baby sister in the eyes, my baby sister who looks just like our mother.

"I need you to listen to me, Yuri. The world out there is different from our own. I am already so lost. I can't bear to drag you down with me. Someday you can decide for yourself to leave," I say. She embraces me and cries into my neck.

"I love you, big brother."

"I love you, too." I look at her one last time and I run in the direction of the village.

CHAPTER SIX

Enlightenment

As the sun rises in the east it casts indigo shadows on the mountains. I walked all night as I did the day I fled from the challenge. Birdsongs that started as a whisper are now blaring as the world wakes up. I feel like I'm in a trance as I approach the village.

Circling around the perimeter through the forest I watch the humans with fascination. They are not gods or demons but they are alive and somehow survive in this world. Physically they are weak but they manage to get by as a collective. I think about my people and how I am not a part of anything anymore. From my place in the treeline I can hear somebody yelling.

"Where is the money?" says a booming voice before I hear a sickening thwack.

"I-I don't have it yet," stammers an older man. As I peer through the ferns I see a well dressed man holding the scruff of an elderly man and pushing him to his knees.

"You say that every time and every time you have nothing!" shouts the well dressed man.

"I'm sorry. The season has been bad. I'm trying–"

"I'm tired of your excuses," yells the well dressed man. He punches the old man in the stomach.

"Leave him be," I say. Both the men look up at me with wide eyes. Now that I'm closer I can see that the elderly man's family is watching in horror. I'm sure I must appear frightening to them.

"Go away, demon! Our laws are not your laws," spits the well dressed man. His hair is shaved on the sides and I can see his veins bulging in his temples.

"What do you want?" I ask.

"Not that it's any of your business but this miserable halfwit hasn't paid his dues," he says as he shakes the old man whose skin is so thin the veins run like rivers underneath.

I carry no human money but I see the well dressed man eye my gold pin with the demon wolf insignia.

"Here, take it. But I never want to see you here again." I say as I hold it out to him.

"I own this land. This is my property. Everything and everyone on it is my property," he hisses.

He throws the old man and begins kicking his fragile body. On impulse I grab the well dressed man's collar and get in his face. I'm a head taller than he is and I narrow my eyes at him. He grabs his sword but I knock it out of his hand.

"It's mine now," I growl.

Eye to eye I look into his soul and see that there is nothing there just like my brothers. I squeeze the collar of his shirt tighter.

"Leave. Now," I bark as I toss him.

He scrambles for a moment and grabs his sword with his hands shaking. I throw the gold pin at his feet and he picks it up without breaking eye contact with me. Scurrying away like the rodent he is, he stops only once to turn around and look at me. I don't move until I can no longer see him.

"Are you okay?" I ask the elderly man as I help him to his feet.

"I have suffered worse," he answers.

"Grandfather! You're bleeding," cries a young child that rushes to his side. The gray hair on the back of his neck is tinged with blood.

"Don't worry, little one. I am fine," he says. The child clings to his side and stares up at me with intense curiosity.

"Come inside, Father. I will make you tea and dress your wounds," says the elderly man's daughter. She holds out her arm and he uses it to support himself. Once he is stable she turns to me.

"Thank you for protecting my father," she says. I realize I'm speechless. I haven't socialized with humans and know nothing of their customs. I nod to acknowledge her.

"Please, tell me your name," requests the old man. His voice is hoarse and he begins having a coughing fit.

"My name is Riku."

"Thank you, Riku. I wish I had something to offer you but as you have witnessed I am destitute," he says in between coughs.

"You don't have to give me anything."

"We are all grateful to you. But if I may ask, why did you help us?" asks the woman. Her child hides behind her legs and gawks at me.

"Because I wanted to."

***

Every day I learn something new in the outside world. During the following weeks I am taught about poverty and what it's like to struggle physically. Demons risk succumbing to the darkness of their demonic rage but humans are struck with illnesses beyond my imagination: sickly coughs and fevers that burn them from the inside, bones that don't heal, and old age. Somehow amidst their shortcomings they are resilient.

They teach me that there is strength in weakness. Although their lives are short they achieve more than I ever have. They know how to be lost. They can survive their limitations and feel so deeply. My father and Ryo said they were no more than ants but that's not true. I can see now that it is us who are the ants, following blind instinct, and ravaging the mountains. Humans have individual needs and wants, no person is the same. It's chaotic but exciting to me.

I ponder our culture and our ways. Everything is for the collective and we are expected to obey a book no one understands. I wonder who I am now that I'm alone. My brother's voice rings in my ears, "A stray, a runt, a brother, who am I to you?"

"No one."

I am reminded of my sister. How she could loathe me but still be disappointed I gave up the throne. She called me a truly beautiful killer, the highest compliment in her eyes.

"The King is God. God is everything. Nothing without you," Rena's crisp voice repeating the demonic canon is stuck in my head. I kneel by the stream and splash water on my face and run it through my hair hoping to drown it out.

Night arrives and with it the howling of wolves. The wind carries their cries to me. I travel further from the mountains to put distance between me and the horrible sound. I've passed six villages, all varying in size and people. I keep my eye out for those who may be in trouble. The demon world is difficult but so is the human world. They are not needy or helpless but I find their conflicts strange. Most of them have to do with money or each other. I smell a demon nearby and scan the perimeter of the village I'm traveling by to make sure Kasai isn't there. So far I haven't seen him since the first time I left the mountain.

"Hey pretty boy," purrs a deep voice from up in the tree.

A man with red hair and black markings on his face is hanging from a branch in front of me. His skin is fair like mine. We have similar facial features. Our eyes are different colors but the same shape.

He has a striped tail that makes swishing noises as he waves it back and forth. I look up at him but don't say anything. He flips from his place in the tree and lands in front of me with grace. His chest is bare and so are his feet. He has black markings on his wrists, whorls going up his arms. They wind around his elbow and stop at his shoulders.

"I haven't seen you around here. Who are you?" he asks as he circles me.

"No one," I reply. This answer amuses him and he cackles. His wildcat vocal cords trill in his throat.

"Don't be coy. Tell me your name," he demands.

"My name is Riku."

"Oh, I know you. The wolf prince from the north. What are you doing away from the pack? I didn't think your people ever came down from the mountain," he says.

"Are you always this interested in the affairs of wolf demons?"

"Only when they concern you," he says, slow and drawn out.

"My reputation precedes me."

"Is it true that you can transform into a wolf so massive it towers over the cedars?"

His tongue touches the roof of his mouth and clicks.

"Why do you care?" I ask.

"I have only heard legends. Maybe someday I will get to see it for myself. Take care pretty boy," he says as he vanishes into the brush.

Besides Kasai I've never spoken with other types of demons before. Most have resorted to the darkness and have lost their speech like the boar. Every day in the outside world I learn not only about humans but also demons. Our teachings on the mountain have left me hungry to know more about where we came from and why we did not retreat with the gods thousands of years ago.

Up ahead I hear voices and catch the scent of another demon. Humans don't often wander into the dark forest and I search for them. It sounds like a man and a woman speaking. I hope it's not Kasai. As I get closer to the sound I see an unusual scene. It's a young woman in the arms of a demon. He and I have the same snow white hair and gold eyes. I draw my sword as I near them assuming there must be something wrong. Peering closer I see that the woman is smiling and she caresses his face in the caring way only a woman in love would do. He whispers something in her ear and she laughs.

I am dumbfounded by what I see. I have been under the impression that humans and demons live in different worlds and never thought about the possibility of them merging. This is a private moment and I should go but I don't move. The young woman's smile is joyous and her face is free of any fear. The demon looks at her as though there is no one else.

"He's waking up," she whispers to him.

She reaches behind her and to my surprise it's a baby. It starts to fuss and the demon takes him from her and begins to rock the child in his arms.

"There, there, my beautiful boy," coos the demon.

The young woman scoots closer to him and they admire their baby together. I feel a twinge in my chest. The demon hands him back to the young woman and she kisses his forehead. Staring at her child she looks like the happiest person in the world.

"I love you," says the demon as he puts his arm around her.

"I love you," she whispers back.

The man wraps himself around her protectively, reassuring her through his touch. Her eyes are on their baby but his eyes are on her. She says something to him in a voice so soft I can't make out their meaning but assume it's sweet from the slight smile he's wearing.

The woman leans into him and he brings her closer to his side. His hand on her hand. Their eyes this time find each other. A light laugh escapes her and the demon seems somehow entranced but unable to invoke the sound himself so he smiles.

I've watched enough and I slink back into the shadows where I contemplate the union of humans and demons.

***

The season has changed and with it brings new hardships for the humans. The mountains to the north and west capture the clouds, restricting the rainfall in the valley. There are periods of rain but this summer's harsh heat cooks the crops in the dirt and the plants crumble and turn to ash. The ground is cracked and dry. No matter how hard they try, nothing will grow. Not every village is unfortunate but many are small with few resources. The rain makes it to the villages close to the mountains but the middle of the valley receives very little. I stay in the shade of the cedars but close enough to see the village beyond the treeline.

"Don't! Please, let her go," a voice cries.

There it is, that scent again. Kasai reeks of death and toxicity. I get there and the fire demon has a young woman in his arms. Three men around her age are reaching for her but Kasai looms over them and pulls her away.

"A deal is a deal," he sings.

"She was desperate! We would rather eat the dirt. Please, let my sister go," says the older boy.

"It's okay, Souta. I made the deal and now I pay the price," says the young woman. Her voice is bold despite her worried expression.

"You heard her. I'll have her back by sundown tomorrow," laughs Kasai. The youngest brother grabs his sister's hand but Kasai knocks him away with minimal effort.

"Let her go," I bark. The fire demon turns around to look me up and down with a smirk.

"What do we have here? A stray," he says.

"Let her go," I repeat.

"Never," he hisses as he sticks his serpent tongue in her mouth and grabs her breast.

I bring my blade down on him but he catches it between two fingers. It doesn't even leave a dent in his skin.

"Your sword was forged in the volcano with hellfire. My body was fortified in the depths of The Underworld. It will have no effect on me," he says.

With one swift motion he flings the sword out from my grip. I rush at him but he kicks me down and to my chagrin I yelp. He stands over me while I lay on the ground and steps on my hand. It's rare for wolf demon bones to break. It takes monumental effort to fracture our bones but he turns mine into dust as he digs in his heel. I hold back an agonizing scream and instead grit my teeth.

It's been over thirty years but I still recall the pain that stained my face the day Ryo broke my nose. He and I were sparring, testing each other, and at the time it was becoming obvious he was falling out of favor with our father and that I would be chosen for the challenge. Rage blazed through him, his eyes boiling red, and once he was on top of me he wouldn't let me up. He just kept smashing my face in with is fist. Over and over again.

Kasai takes only a second to grind my bones so fine my hand hangs as though it were filled with sand.

"I do whatever I want, take whatever I want, when I want," he says as he walks into the woods with the young woman in his arms.

The middle brother helps me sit up and we both look at my hand that now hangs at an unnatural angle from my wrist. He rips a portion of his obi and wraps my palm. It reminds me of Yahei.

"I'm sorry I can't do more for you," he says as he ties the bandage.

"I wish I could have helped your sister," I reply. The oldest brother is at my side helping me to my feet while the youngest brother stares into the forest where his sister was taken.

"No one has ever tried to stand up to Kasai," says the oldest brother.

"My name is Akai," says the middle brother, "and this is Souta," he motions to the oldest brother.

"Over there is Masa," says Souta pointing to the little brother whose eyes do not leave the treeline.

"My name is Riku."

"Thank you for trying to help our sister, Himari," says Akai. I nod to let him know I'm listening but I keep my head down. I've never felt helpless the way I do right now. Kasai's immense strength is intimidating, even to me. As I'm leaving I feel someone tug on my cloak. It's the youngest brother, Masa.

"Please, don't go," he whispers.

"At least stay for the night. It's the summer festival," says Akai.

"I should be going."

"Your hand is badly injured. Rest here with us," suggest Souta.

"Your kindness is wasted on me," I answer.

"You make us feel safe. Please stay a bit longer," begs Masa.

He isn't a child but not quite a man either, somewhere in between. I stand still at his words and the middle brother uses this as an opportunity to guide me.

"Come with me," says Akai as he ushers me towards the festival.

My body heals rapidly but an injury this severe will take time. It throbs and I remove my obi to make a sling for my arm. The sun is setting in the west and the clouds turn milky orange. There is a large bonfire in the middle of the village and musicians playing celebratory songs. In clear containers are captured fireflies and copper urns filled with wildflowers.

Children wear bright colored kimonos and play with spinning tops or chase each other. Women dance with one another while the men sit off to the side and pass a bottle around. Everyone looks happy even though I know Kasai has taken more than just Himari.

Humans try to make the best of hard times. I don't know how they do it. Akai, Souta, and I sit with the men while Masa runs off. All of them stop talking to gape at me.

"This is Riku. He stood up to Kasai," says Souta. The men look at each other and then back at me.

"He tried to get Himari back for us," says Akai with a smile. The men seem to ease at his statement.

"Where do you come from?" asks the man sitting next to Souta.

"The northern mountains," I say.

"You're one of the wolf demons. I didn't think they ever left the pack," says another man.

"We don't." It must be obvious that this is a sore subject for me because they change the topic.

"Here, drink this. It'll make you feel better," says the man sitting next to Souta.

"What is it?" I ask.

"Just drink it, have some fun." I take a drink from the bottle. It's sour but not bad. I hand it back but he pushes it away.

"Have another one," he urges.

To please him I do and Akai takes the bottle from me. The aftertaste is acidic and odd. As it gets darker the music gets louder and the people talk slower. I stand by the fire and keep to myself.

"Drink up, wolf boy!" says an old man with a beard as he pushes a bottle into my unbroken hand.

I don't want to be rude and I know nothing about socializing with humans. I resort to copying what they do. The drink is warm in my stomach. I'm starting to feel strange. My thoughts spin around in a dull haze that is far away from me.

The ache in my hand subsides. I can't feel its thrashing pain. It's there, I know it is, but the feeling is murky. Painful memories and the heat of the injury are no longer bothersome for I no longer care. I don't want to go home but I miss the snow.

Everyone's face is red, their foreheads are covered in perspiration from the dancing, and the warm midsummer air. Their music is foreign to me. It isn't the drums of war or traditional victory music like my people are accustomed to. These songs are played with emotion and creativity.

"Having fun, Riku?" asks Akai. He is panting and swaying as he talks to me. I don't know what to say.

"No? This will help," he says and puts a bottle to my chest.

I take a drink and hand it back. Akai takes a long pull from it, then insists I have another. My vision is blurry and I feel disoriented. I take a step away from the fire and feel my legs buckle. What's happening to me?

"Look, the wolf boy is drunk!" laughs a fat man with a mustache.

Drunk? I've never been drunk. I'm in a daze as their faces fade in and out. The fire turns everything into yellow shadows. I feel their hands on my armor and hear them talking but I can't center myself among all the nameless faces.

Women come up to me and grab my shoulders and run their fingers through my hair. Then they giggle and skip out of my sight. One of them puts her hand on my forehead and pulls my hair back.

"You have beautiful eyes," she says and she kisses me hard on the mouth.

Her lips caress the shell of my ear and she keeps whispering words I can't make out. My armor is weighing me down–no, it's constricting my breath. There are too many things happening at once. Men slap my back and laugh about things I don't understand. They keep trying to get me to drink but I decline. I don't think I like being drunk. There are hands all over me and I struggle to tell what's real and what's not.

"Are you okay, wolf boy?"

"The wolf boy is so drunk he can't even stand up!"

"Give him some space," says Akai but then there is nothing.

A glimpse of white in the dark. Is it the moon? I know there are trees. The scent of cedar and the air before it snows. Branches weave together like black lace over indigo silk. I move closer to what I thought was the moon. It's a deer. She's all white. Her eyes are on me. The mouth opens and I wait for her message but it's interrupted.

I wake up next to the remains of the fire. Akai and Masa are passed out next to me along with a few other men. I'm sick to my stomach and in the back of my head is a pounding headache.

"You're awake," says Souta as he kneels down to shake Masa and Akai.

"I feel horrible," I rasp.

"Sometimes that happens when you drink," he laughs.

"I'm never drinking again," I say and he laughs even more.

"That's what we all say and here we are drinking night after night." He helps me to my feet. Now that I'm alert I notice the pain in my hand and wince.

"I have to go," I announce.

"You are always welcomed in our village, Riku. Be safe out there," says Akai through bleary eyes.

"Thank you," I say. I've never been welcomed anywhere before.

CHAPTER SEVEN

The Girl with Stars on Her Face

It's been seven years since I left my home. I've been on my own long enough that company feels unusual. Time stands still for me. When I visit the villages I see aged faces and funerals. Their lives are beautiful but short. My life is long but empty. I am comforted by my loneliness. If I have nothing then nothing can hurt me.

My vision is clear under the moonless sky. Mice scurry across my path and owls announce their presence as they fly above me. The night flowers are opening, they smell dewy and sweet. Bats call to each other as they weave through the branches in the trees. There are a hundred different sounds in the night: chirping, hissing, and scratching. The forest spirits peek out at me from behind ferns and boulders. They are used to me now and do not hide themselves.

A twig snaps and I catch a glimpse of white. It stops me in my tracks. I wait to see or hear it again. Leaves rustle to my left. There it is again, a drop of milk in the ink. Then it's silent. No insect makes a sound and the birds refuse to flap their wings. Nothing flies above me and the mice retreat into their homes. It rushes past me with such speed it startles me. The hooves hit the ground but make no noise. It's the white deer!

I chase after it. It runs with agility, weaving through the oaks, and the camphor trees. The vision Yama showed me comes to mind and I speed up to keep pace with the mystic creature. The forest spirits line the path we're on, they too, are amazed by the white deer. My heart pounds against my armor and I feel as though it would come out if not for the steel. I lose sight of the deer and panic. Where is she? I scan all around me but there are only red and green reflector eyes from the nightbiters looking back at me.

She jumps out at me from the right and takes off again. I am careful not to lose her this time. I worry that the gods may change their minds and I will never see the deer again. As we run I smell the familiar scent of Kasai, the burning rot. It is followed by the smell of smoke and I know I am close to the place of my destiny. The deer and I exit the forest and come upon a grassy knoll with red spider lilies. I look down to see a village on fire. The deer stands in front of me and stares its otherworldly stare. She wants me to go in.

It starts to rain as I enter the village and I am met with the scent of death. Blood stains the ground purple and it looks bruised. There are bodies everywhere. Limbs are strewn about the ground with reckless abandon. This was Kasai's work. My blood runs hot and boils under my skin but I need to remain calm. I'm looking for something important.

I step through broken homes and destroyed shops. The rice fields are a sea of flames. The fire crackles and pops but it sounds like someone's laughing. I look into the lifeless stares of men, women, and children. A man with a baby in his arms lies on the blood soaked grass. I wish I got here sooner. It looks like everyone is dead. Maybe the deer was wrong or perhaps it is not a messenger at all.

"No! Father, please. Please come back to me," says a small voice.

I turn the corner to see a young girl kneeling with her father's hand in hers. He is split at the torso and his intestines are stretched across the dirt.

There is the long shadow of a man approaching her. It's Kasai, he's wearing the head of the bear over his face as a hood. Only his mouth and chin are visible. Even at this distance I can see his tongue slither over his teeth as he approaches her. The smirk on his face is perverse. Either she doesn't see Kasai's shadow or she doesn't care, she remains on her knees holding her father's hand. I run across the village and grab her. She looks up at me with eyes so dark they are almost black.

"We have to go," I say.

"Who are you?" she asks. I can hear Kasai behind me.

"No one."

I need to get her away from him as fast as I can. The white deer bounds in front of me again. It leaps into the trees and I follow her.

"Give her to me! She's mine," snarls Kasai. I look down to see that she is unconscious. I'm glad she doesn't have to hear him.

"She's mine! She's always been mine!" he shouts.

I can't put enough distance between us. He's too close. There is a river next to me and I get an idea. I use the same trick I used on Ryo and I run through the river to cover my tracks. The deer stays to my right and we run next to each other.

"Come back here!" yells Kasai.

His voice is further away this time. To my relief there is a waterfall coming down from a small cliff. I shield her with my cloak and walk through the clear curtain. Pressing my back against the wall I watch Kasai nearing us. Every step he takes burns the grass and leaves soot. I already know my weapon is useless against him. If he finds us I'll have to run. I could try and take him on in my transformed state but I don't trust myself with the girl in my demonic body.

If he wants her he's going to have to pry her from my cold, dead hands. I'm shocked at my assertion. Kasai walks back and forth but doesn't attempt to look past the waterfall. He scales the cliff and is out of sight. Kasai knows her scent and I take off my cloak and wrap it around her. She smells like tea leaves and honey. He knows my scent as well. I pull mud up from the bottom of the river and rub it on my legs and the back of my neck.

I step out from our hiding place and look around to make sure he isn't lurking nearby. The white deer is waiting for me and after she notices I see her she bounds off into the forest. I run with her all night. Soon dawn approaches and I feel the girl stirring in my cloak.

I see a village up ahead. The deer stops at the treeline and stares at me. I peer down the hill to inspect the place. It is twice as large as most villages I've seen. The temple is sizable and in the fields grow plentiful rice and root vegetables. This village appears to be wealthier than the others. Down by the shrines I see a young priestess with red trousers and a paper ribbon in her hair. She is praying. Her face is serious but has a hint of sweetness to it. The deer nudges me with her nose and I follow her to a spring that's behind the temple. The grass is lush and dark green here.

The sun is rising. I unwrap my cloak and lay her down in the softest part of the grass. I brush her long hair out of her face. Now that I really see her I notice she has an interesting pattern of freckles across the bridge of her nose and cheeks. It's in the shape of the constellation Gemini. She has a dainty nose and a rose colored mouth. Her eyebrows are thin. She flutters her eyelashes that are so long they touch her cheeks. I flinch at the sight. Then I hear people waking in the village and retreat into the camphors and hydrangeas.

The light cast a white circle around the girl. It almost appears as an ethereal glow. A man exits the temple and runs towards her. From the blue robes and jewelry he wears I see he is a monk. His face is soft and kind. Kneeling down he lifts up the girl and gently shakes her. He looks into the forest right in the direction I am and I swear he sees me even though I'm hidden in the shadows. Again he gently shakes the girl. His eyes are wet.

"Open your eyes," he whispers. The girl remains unmoving in his arms. A tear rolls down his face onto the girl's nose.

"Please," he says, "please, open your eyes."

I am confused and look over to the white deer. What does it want from me? Is this my destiny or coincidence? The monk lifts up her chin to get a better look at her.

"Open your eyes," he whispers once again. This time the girl's eyebrows furrow before she wakes up.

"There you are," smiles the monk. The girl stares up at him with a blank gaze.

"Lady Kiyori! Lady Kiyori, come quick!" cries the monk over his shoulder.

After a moment the priestess I saw earlier is at the girl's side. Her expression is a mix of shock and awe.

"Where did she come from?" she asks the monk.

"From the heavens."

The priestess runs into the temple and calls for help. Two younger priestesses follow behind her, their long hair waving back and forth. The girl watches everything going on but doesn't say anything. The deer takes off and the monk looks in my direction again. This time I swear he makes eye contact with me.

****

Three summers have passed since I saw the girl with the freckles or Kasai. If my destiny was to save her then I hope I have fulfilled my sister's prophecy. As I think of my sister and the vision she had I hear a howl in the distance. I never respond, only listen. They stopped cursing my name years ago. This isn't just any howl though, it's Yama. I stop walking and listen for her.

"Yuri has left the mountain," she says.

This makes me laugh. My baby sister was right, we did have the same heart. I assume she has gone to live with the human boy in the village. She will protect them. I haven't laughed or smiled in an eternity but the news of my baby sister's decision to abandon everything we ever knew wakes emotions I haven't allowed myself to have. Yuri has always been bright. I remember her words, "I can't turn a blind eye. If we do not witness any suffering but our own, how can we know who we truly are?"

I didn't understand it at the time but now I do. We are a brutal people but life for the humans is just as harsh if not harsher. They have little time, few resources, and they fall prey to the demons that differ from me and Yuri. Yama howls again. I can't comprehend her message which is only two words.

"Now, Riku."

Now? Now what? I scan the area looking for a clue and before I see it I know she's there, it's the white deer. She bounds past me without stopping and I chase after her. This time she doesn't stop for me or turn around. I wonder what could be so urgent. We run until the sun is high in the sky and the heat is at its peak. The familiar scent of camphors and hydrangeas tint the air but there's more to it. It's the sweet fragrance of honey and green tea leaves.

The deer slows and we walk in the shade of the camphors. I hear someone singing. It's not high or silvery like most women's. It's a low and husky tone.

Was it you, was it you
Who hid me in the tree? Covered me in leaves
There was a man

I know he came for me The smoke hides his face
Even in my dreams Who was he, who was he

I get as close as I can without revealing myself. There's a young woman with shiny black hair that contrasts against her yellow kimono. She's faced away from me picking flowers. I wait eagerly for her to turn around but I already know who she is. I can see her weaving the stems together. She makes a necklace of white baby roses and as she places them around herself she looks towards the forest.

I'm disappointed to see her wearing a frown. It seems wrong for such a beautiful person to look sad the way she does. Making her way towards the treeline I worry she may have seen me. She finds a patch of shade that's right in front of my hiding place and she sings about me in her haunting voice.

Was it you, was it you
Who left me by the spring?There was a man
I know he saved me but
I see him only in my dreams Was it you, was it you
Who left me by the spring

I back away startled and step on a twig that snaps under my boot. She looks up from her flower necklace and stares into the forest. The air in my lungs turns chilly in the summer heat and I feel like I can't breathe. She goes back to plucking at the grass and picking petals off the flowers one by one. A girl her age with a widow's peak and dark blue eyes runs up to hug her and I see the girl with freckles smile for the first time. Her friend whispers something to her and they both throw up their heads and laugh. Good, maybe she is happy after all.

A young man is approaching them. He appears to be a few years older than her. His hair is short, his eyebrows are thick, and his eyes are violet. The girl with the widow's peak whispers in her ear again and runs off back towards the village. The young man has something behind his back and she looks up at him with an expression I can't read. I can tell he is in love with her.

He holds a bouquet of bright colored lilies and hands them to her. The girl looks shocked by his gesture. Kneeling down next to her he says something in a hushed voice but I can't make out what it is. She looks at her flowers and back and him and shakes her head "no." The man smiles a disappointed grin but he still looks at her with tenderness.

"I'm sorry," she says. The man takes her hands in his and looks down.

"It's okay. Really, it is. Just know that I am here for you," he says.

She has tears building in her lash line but they do not fall. Her bottom eyelashes hold back the rain. They are bold and dark. As he heads back towards the village she stares at the lilies he gave her with a pouty face. I've made a habit out of watching too many private moments and I scold myself to leave. I can't though because she keeps singing.

Was it you, was it you
Who left me by the spring?
I know your face
But not your name
I've been wondering
Who was he, who was he

"My name is Riku," I think to myself as I watch her leave. She doesn't bring the lilies the man gave her and for some reason I find solace in this.

***

The seasons change and the years go by but time is meaningless to me. It's been years since I heard her haunting song but I can't get it out of my head. I've put a great deal of distance between me and that village. I think it's indecent of me to spy on her like I did that day. Yama knew the deer was there and urged me to follow it. What does it all mean? I still don't understand. Her visions are cryptic and confusing.

I try not to think about her but she is on my mind often. She is a stranger to me but I feel a connection to her beyond the white deer's message and my sister's prophecy. We are both fatherless outsiders. I don't know the girl I saved, but her pain is my pain.

By now she's probably changed her mind and decided to marry the man with violet eyes. I wish for her happiness. Seeing her friend make her laugh comforts me but the pangs of guilt hit me in the stomach when I remember her sad pouty face. There is a howl in the distance that turns my blood to ice. It's Yama howl and what she says freezes me in place.

"She's looking for you, Riku." I knew she remembered me by the song she sang but I never would have guessed she would seek me out.

"She needs you. Go to her," Yama's howl rings out over the valley.

I sprint through the woods towards the direction of her village. She couldn't have gone too far from there. Thinking of all the demons and dangerous things that exist in my world brings on a wave of dread. Humans are vulnerable and knowing Kasai could find her out here forces me to run faster. She's been fortunate to not have been found already. I remember the first human I spoke to and what he said, that Kasai was from The Underworld and all his deals are absolute.

I'm crashing through the forest in a reckless manner. Pieces of ferns and small branches fall in my wake. The thought of Kasai's tongue in her mouth horrifies me and I don't know what I will do if he should find her.

"Hey there, pretty boy."

The tiger demon is looking down at me from his perch in a tree. He's grooming his claws and smiling that smug grin of his. "I see you're in a hurry. What's the rush?" he asks.

"I'm looking for someone," I answer.

"Everybody is looking for someone," he sighs.

"Have you seen a young woman here in the forest?" I ask.

"I see lots of women," he says with a wink.

"Did you see a woman with long dark hair and freckles come through here?" I ask. This gets his attention.

"As a matter of fact I did. That's funny! She said she was looking for a man," he cackles his wildcat laugh.

"Which way did she go?"

"Oh, I don't know. I wasn't really paying attention," he says and throws his hands up.

"Dammit, tell me which way she went!"

"The wolf prince has a temper just like the girl! You two are meant to be."

"What do you mean?" I ask.

"Well, she drew her weapon at me rather quickly. Wasn't very nice or smiley either," he huffs. His answer pleases me but I try not to show it.

"Are you going to tell me where she went or not?" I ask as I reach for my blade.

"Calm down, calm down. No need to hack me to pieces, I was just having some fun! She went north."

"Thank you," I say before taking off towards the mountains I swore I'd never go near again.

Evening is almost here and I search everywhere for her. The tiny demons that gather in hordes get stronger at night and become more persistent. My boots pound the dry summer dirt and I kick up a cloud of dust behind me. I'm running out of daylight. The sun is a sliver on the horizon. The fragrant scent of honey and tea leaves is potent here, she has to be close. Then I hear it. She's calling my name.

I'm nearing the cliff and I see her at the edge being swarmed by the rodent and insect demons. She holds a sword in her right and a small knife in her left but there are too many of them. One of the nightbiters lunges at her and knocks her off the cliff.

I can't let her die. I jump after her into the ravine. Her hair is a curtain of black ink as she falls. I pull her close as I brace for the landing. Wolf demon bones can withstand a fall from a height like this. I land on my feet and leave a small crater in the gorge. The dust settles around us and I pull back her black hair. She's unconscious but okay.

The sound of a thousand fluttering wings and scratching legs hover above. The nightbiters are following us. I rush through the gully, up to the other side, and run until I no longer hear the chirps of the tiny demons behind me. Now that she's safe I realize how tired I am. I sit against the trunk of a tree and lean my head back and look up at the stars. They remind me of her freckles.

I thought I only blinked but I must have fallen asleep because suddenly I feel the sun on my face. At first I'm confused by the weight in my lap but I open my eyes to see she's still sleeping in my arms. I set her down to splash water on my face and collect my thoughts. Why is she looking for me?

I see her stirring. It looks like she's having a nightmare. Beads of sweat form on her forehead and she claws at the grass beneath her. I kneel by her and hold her hand. She squeezes it and clenches her teeth. I wish she would wake up. Almost as though granting my wish she opens her dark eyes and looks up at me.

"Riku?" she asks.

"How do you know my name?"

"I see you every night in my dreams," she says.

"What are you doing out here?"

"Looking for you," she answers. I am baffled but intrigued by her.

"Here. Drink this," I say and offer her water. She takes a few sips and coughs.

"Thank you," she says.

"Why are you looking for me?" I ask.

I could stare down Ryo and Rena but I can't handle her dark mystifying gaze so I get up and look towards my old home.

"I need your help. A giant centipede has taken over my village. We can't fight him. Please, Riku."

"Why my help?" I ask.

I'm perplexed as to how she knows my name and even more confused by her willingness to come all the way out here to get me. She clutches the water container and stares at the ground.

"Do you remember me?" she asks. I could never forget her.

"Yes," I say.

"I know I should be thankful and I have no right to ask you but I need to know. Why did you save me all those years ago?" she asks.

I wonder if she knows about Kasai. Humans are aware of demons and spirits of the forest but they do not know our laws or our ways. I don't expect her to understand my sister's vision or our people's brutal traditions.

"I was in the forest near your village when I smelled the fire. It was too late by the time I got there. Almost everything had been destroyed. I was about to leave but I saw Kasai, a fire demon who enjoys playing games with humans. He preys on the weakness in people's hearts. I couldn't let him take you," I say.

"You brought me to Lady Kiyori and Brother Minoru's village because you wanted me to be safe. You must have chosen them for a reason. They raised me well and took care of me. Please, help me save them."

She thinks I'm going to say "no" but I would never deny her of anything.

"Were you happy there?" I ask. This question seems to surprise her.

"Yes, I was happy. My family is irreplaceable but they took me in as their sister, daughter, and friend. Look," she says as she takes off her bracelet and places it in my palm. It's real gold, expensive. Inside is a small engraving, it says "cherished."

"Cherished," I say to myself. She was loved.

"Will you help me defeat the centipede?" she asks.

I turn the bracelet over in my hand and think about the monk who spoke to her with such kindness. His face was wet with tears when she didn't open her eyes. I remember how the priestesses hovered over her with worried expressions. They kept her safe all these years. She loves them enough to risk her life searching for me.

"Let's go," I say and start walking in the direction of her village.

CHAPTER EIGHT

What I Carry

She is different from the other women I've met. We have walked all day without much conversation. It's not that I don't want to talk to her but I don't know what to say. I still can't believe she's here. I catch glimpses of her behind me. She folds her arms and frowns as she looks everywhere but me. I wish to get her attention but I don't even know her name. I pause on the path and she bumps into me.

"Oh, sorry. What is it, Riku?" she asks and backs up right away.

"I never asked you your name."

"My name is Aiya," she says.

Her name is pretty, like her. We continue on the trail a bit further. I notice she is tired but she won't say so. There is a field of wildflowers up ahead and I suggest we take a break there. I lean against the trunk of a tree and she walks into the meadow and disappears in the tall grass that comes up to her knees.

I stay in the shade and contemplate our intertwined fate. Yama told me about the vision over a decade ago. When she said I was carrying something precious in my cloak I imagined an object, not a person. I don't know if I am up to this challenge either. The thought of failing her gnaws at my conscience. She hasn't sat up in a while. I go to check on her and find her asleep in the white flowers. It appears she's having another nightmare and I think of her song.

Was it you, was it you

Who hid me in the tree
Covered me in leaves
There was a man
I know he came for me
The smoke hides his face
Even in my dreams
Who was he, who was he

Kasai is from The Underworld and I wonder if he has the ability to invade her dreams. I don't like the idea of his lips on hers or his grasp on her mind. From her mouth escapes the horrible sound of grinding teeth. She turns to her side and claws at the ground. I can tell she's fighting the nightmare but it weighs heavy on her heart. I reach down and put my hand under her chin and try to get her to relax her jaw.

"Aiya," I call her name softly in hopes of waking her up without disturbing her. Tears fall down her face and soak her long eyelashes.

"Aiya," I say again. She coughs and I pull back my hand.
"I must have fallen asleep," she mumbles as she rubs her eyes and looks at the wetness on her hand.

"Aiya, I've been wanting to tell you something."

"What is it?" she asks as she looks up at me with eyes so deep I could fall in.

"I'm sorry. I wish I reached your village sooner," I confess.

"It's not your fault, Riku."

"I know." To Aiya, I am a stranger, but to me she is my destiny, and I ponder what the gods have in store for us.

"It was my father who brought the fire demon," she starts, "his crops went bad. Kasai offered him a solution but in return he wanted me. On the day Kasai was supposed to collect me, my father changed his mind. This enraged him and he burned the village to the ground."

I hold my fist and try to hide my anger. Kasai's viciousness is alarming and my weapon won't work against him. I don't know what I'm going to do should he come for her. It could be my imagination but I think I smell the burning rot of the fire demon. I scan the area feeling as though we are being watched.

"We better get going," I say and help her to her feet.

***

I tell Aiya we should travel through the night. She looks into the blue and black woods with that unreadable expression. I hold out my hand to her.

"I'll guide you. I can see in the dark," I say. Her slender fingers grip my palm and we venture into the forest. An owl flies overhead and dives in front of us to pick off a small mouse. Slowing my pace so that she can keep up I notice a blur of something white. It's her again, the white deer. She stops and stares at me for a moment before running off. A twig snaps and I feel Aiya squeeze my hand as she lets out a frightened gasp.

"It's okay. It's just a deer," I assure her.

We exit the treeline and stand at a cliff that faces the northern mountains. Yama must know I'm looking at them because she howls my name. This interests Aiya and I see her look at me and then the mountains.

"Do you ever answer?" she asks.

"No," I reply.

"What happened there?" She stares at them and I wonder how much of my world she understands. I decide to be honest with her.

"Wolf demons have kept the tradition of killing the alpha to ascend to the throne. My father got too old and he chose me to lead. I refused and it was my older brother that took over. He resented me for not fulfilling our father's wishes. My brother challenged me and I declined. My siblings began abusing me soon after," I say.

"Why did you refuse?"

"I had no interest in leading. I didn't want to kill my father or fight my brother." Not wanting to remember my past I turn away to leave but Yama howls again for me again.

"Watch over her, Riku. She is the one," she says.

I hear Aiya stumble from fatigue. I know she wants her independence but I can't watch her go on like this.

"Here. Let me carry you," I say and kneel down for her to get on my back.

"You don't have to do that. I'm fine," she says as I knew she would. We are both stubborn.

"You're exhausted and you can't see in the dark. Let me help you," I say and realize I may have been too aggressive.

"Okay," she whispers and puts her arms around my neck.

Her long hair falls over my shoulder and she rests her hand where my heart is. I haven't had anybody this close to me in a long time. She breathes warm air into my ear and her legs drape around me. I almost forgot what it's like to touch someone. I don't think she means to but she falls asleep.

I feel more secure this way. It's difficult for me to exist in front of people. Over the years I've assisted a dozen human families in need but I do not fit in. Most of the women in the villages call me "shy." I am not afraid but I don't know what to say, especially to Aiya. She is a mystery to me. All night I contemplate what the white deer is trying to tell me and I question what I am to Aiya. Am I her friend, her savior, or no one?

It's morning but she is still fast asleep. I don't mind carrying her so I let her rest. The nightbiters retreat into the deeper parts of the woods and the birds cry out to wake everything up. I pick up the faint scent of a demon but it's not Kasai. I think I smell a cat.

"Riku?" she says my name in her husky voice and I stop to put her down.

"Why didn't you wake me?" she asks.

"You needed rest," I say.

"Thank you."

As we walk, Aiya combs her hair with her fingers and stretches. She covers her mouth to yawn. I've always thought she was beautiful but this is the first time I think I've really seen her.

"There you are. My little mouse," purrs a familiar voice from up in the tree.

"Go away," she says and shoos him.

I stop and lock my eyes on the tiger demon. His predatory gaze on her makes me want to rip out his wildcat vocal cords with my teeth. I think he's doing it to aggravate me because he turns in my direction with a smirk.

"I see you found your man," he teases as his tail slashes the air. Aiya speeds up but calls over her shoulder to him.

"What I do is none of your business," she shouts.

"Suit yourself. You smell like a dog now anyway," he says.

He turns his nose up at me and licks his lips before slinking away. I know I have no right to be but I am jealous. More jealous than when I saw Ryo's hands on Hoshi. Aiya is ahead of me with her arms crossed and her head down. It's obvious that the tiger demon upset her.

"What was that all about?" I ask as I approach her side.

"Nothing. Just a creepy cat is all," she says.

I don't take Aiya for a liar but she's not telling me something. She keeps her head down as she walks. My staring is probably making her uncomfortable. I take the lead and she follows me.

***

In this part of the forest the bamboo grows taller than the cedars and oak trees. We wander through the maze's twist and turns. There is a slight rustling beyond the walls but I brush it off. We are nearing her village and I think about the task before me. To defeat the giant centipede I'll have to transform. I haven't done so since the final war I fought with my father.

Last time I was in my wolf state the boar provoked me and I lost myself to the darkness. If that happens while I'm fighting the centipede I'm in danger of harming the village or worse, her. She needs me to do this. I can't let her down. Aiya's footsteps have stopped and she is looking down one of the tunnels of the maze.

"Aiya! Don't fall behind," I call.

"I'll be right there," she says and runs to catch up to me.

I take us down a dead end and out of the corner of my eye I see shiny black hair dart across the bamboo maze.

"Did you see that?" she asks.

"I did," I say and draw my sword. I motion for her to stay close to me as I peek around the corner.

"Who is she?" she asks.

"I don't know. Stay next to me," I order her.

We take a hard left and run. There is no scent of a demon but something is here. Why can't I smell it though? I feel the ground vibrate and hear the sound of laughter. I can't tell which way it is coming from but when I turn around I see Aiya isn't behind me anymore. As I'm running back the way we came I spot her but before I can get there a net is cast over her and she is pulled out of my sight.

I should have kept a better eye on her. There is a loud roar and the earth shakes causing the bamboo stalks to quiver. Turning the corner I see Aiya in front of a giant spider demon emerging from the ground. It's dragging her in its web towards its mouth. That is why I couldn't sense it. If an orb spider lives to be four-hundred years old it's given unique abilities. This one can disguise its demonic aura. It dwells underground and reveals itself once its prey is near. On top of its head is the female puppet it uses as a lure.

It roars, spitting venom. The creature is repulsive with a dozen red eyes and long jagged black legs. Standing on its back legs it roars again. Aiya is struggling in its web and as the creature comes down I rush past her and drive my blade in its head. I dig in my sword, scrambling its brain, and it collapses. I allow myself a sigh of relief. That was too close.

"Are you okay?" I ask and cut her out of the web. She doesn't say anything but nods. Not caring if she perceives my actions as too aggressive I grab her hand and keep her next to me until we're out of the spider's den. I won't let anything like that happen ever again.

We come by a river and Aiya says she's going to get some water. I give her time to herself and I stay by the wisteria trees to survey our surroundings. Someone calls her name and she looks up. Across the river I see a young woman with red and black ears on top of her head. It's a fox demon.

"Aiya! Is it really you?"

"Hanako!"

"Aiya, you're okay! I was so worried I'd never see you again," says the fox girl. I make my way to them and see she is crying on Aiya's shoulder.

"We're together now. That's all that matters," says Aiya.

As I approach the fox girl looks at me with wide eyes. If I'm not mistaken this is the western fox princess. I've heard rumors of her kindness towards humans. This eases me and I feel better knowing Aiya had someone to protect her.

She has shimmery starlight hair and curious chestnut eyes that look at me with bewilderment. Her face is round and her lips are light pink making her appear quite young. As I near I see she has short feathery eyelashes.

"You found him," she whispers.

"More like he found me," laughs Aiya.

"Riku, this is Hanako. She helped me when I first began my journey. Her cleverness saved me from Kasai," she says.

I didn't know other demons felt protective of humans. She gives me a polite bow before speaking.

"I have to tell you something, Aiya." Her expression changes and her ears go flat against her head.

"After you and I were separated I saw Kasai looking for you. He was getting too close so I shapeshifted and mimicked your voice. I lured him as far to the south as I could. I came back to get you but you were gone. I followed your scent to the cliff. I thought you were dead," she cries. Aiya strokes her starlight hair.

"It's okay, Hanako. I'm right here," says Aiya. Her frown is back.

"Your village is close. We should continue," I say.

"Thank you for taking care of Aiya. She is like a sister to me," says Hanako.

The fox girl smiles at me with genuine warmth and refuses to let go of Aiya's hand. I don't know Hanako, but her heart is my heart.

I walk in front while they follow behind. Hanako is very talkative and clings to Aiya. She doesn't seem to mind and listens eagerly to her friend's effervescent chatter with their elbows locked. Hanako isn't shy about showing Aiya how much she loves her and I get an ache in my chest. The sky is turning indigo black and I kneel to carry Aiya.

"Hanako, can you see in the dark?" I ask.

"You bet," she answers in a cheery voice.

We walk in silence most of the night. I look over periodically to see Hanako picking flowers and putting them in her hair and dancing to music that isn't there. I'm happy Aiya has someone sweet in her life. I wonder who else is this kind hearted and carefree. The clever fox bested Kasai and I smile at the thought of her fooling him.

Aiya's cheek rests against my neck and I listen to the soft breaths that escape her pouty mouth. I am careful not to scratch her with my claws and notice how icy cold my hands feel on her thighs. Hanako mimics the songs of midnight birds and they sing back to her. She jumps and claps her hands when they reply. I haven't been around fox demons but I have heard of their strange magic that is based in illusion, not strength. Her ability to trick Kasai is impressive.

Aiya must be having another dream because I feel hot tears on the back of my neck. I curse the fire demon for bringing her so much misery. Her father's betrayal disgusts me. Thinking about her holding his lifeless hand as I grabbed her stops me in my tracks.

"Do you see something, Riku?" asks Hanako.

"It's Aiya. She cries in her sleep," I say.

"Aiya puts on a brave face but she carries a lot of hurt," says Hanako.

I push the thought of Aiya's father out of my mind and keep walking. I want to hate him for his weakness but I have seen their weakness in the villages and I have been weak myself.

The fox girl continues, "The first time I saw Aiya, I was mesmerized by her. I thought she must be very courageous to come out this far. I was curious why such a pretty girl would be in the middle of the forest and I followed her. After she sensed my presence she threw a rock at me! It's a funny story now that I think about it," says Hanako with a giggle.

"I heard someone calling my name. I got there just in time, Aiya was being attacked by a horde of nightbiters. They ambushed her and she fell off the cliff. She didn't cry then," I say.

"I'm glad you found her," says Hanako in a considerate tone.

I haven't allowed myself to think about it until now and it hits me with such ferocity my eyes water. I'm more than glad I found her. I love her. I have loved her since the day I heard her sing about me. I tell myself she is my destiny, but she has been my everything. Yama's vision didn't prepare me for this. The fox girl can see my tears but pretends she doesn't.

"Me too," I say.

***

The demonic aura surrounding the village is a heavy cloak that reeks of toxicity. I hate this smell. It reminds of the boar demons and Kasai. They share the same rotten black blood. Hanako wrinkles up her nose at the smell and her ears twitch. She can sense the evil here, too. Aiya walks next to me with that unreadable expression but I know she is worried.

The mist has subdued everything in this part of the forest and nothing stirs. I pretend to be dauntless even though I'm terrified of succumbing to the darkness. I motion for Aiya and Hanako to stop. As I walk towards the village I hear her call my name. It sounds translucent in her mouth.

"Riku!"

"What is it, Aiya?"

"I just wanted to say thank you."

I look at her and tell myself to remember her face when the rage overcomes me. Then I disappear into the fog. The swirling mist stings my eyes with its acrid scent. I grit my teeth and prepare to transform for the first time since I left home.

My tongue bleeds as my canines elongate and my spine shatters. My bones are reshaping under the skin. There is pressure in my chest where my sternum breaks and my hip bones shift. Muscle, sinew, and cartilage tear as the transformation completes. I roar to wake the centipede that's burrowed beneath the village.

"Go away you mangy mutt," it hisses.

The beast lunges at me but I dodge it. I paw at him and knock his face into the dirt. The ground shakes and cedars fall as he dislodges himself. He uncoils his massive body from the village to fight me. I pounce but he flings me off of him.

"You want to play? Then die!" it shouts at me as it aims to strike.

With an enormous amount of force he hits me right in the nose and I yelp in pain. This pleases the awful creature and its body vibrates with laughter.

"Bad dog," it taunts. I feel the demonic rage threaten to take over. We circle each other and I keep Aiya's face in the back of my mind. The air shifts and I rush at the centipede and tear out a large chunk of flesh from his trunk.

"What are you doing? No!" it wails.

I run the perimeter of the village and hack the creature into bits with my jaw. Black blood drips from my teeth and burns my throat. I don't stop even though it leaves lesions on the roof of my mouth. It blisters my gums and the inside of my cheeks.

The centipede attempts to lunge at me again but he is missing too much of his body to raise himself from the ground. I step on the beast's face and rip out his throat, flinging black blood onto the tops of the trees. It sizzles where it lands. I hear him sigh and his body deflates. Purple and black mist evaporate from his wounds and his body disintegrates. A hundred serrated legs go limp and dissipate into nothingness.

I remember Aiya's hand on my heart, how my name sounds in her mouth, and it brings me back. Picking up the remains of the centipede I pull his toxic body away from the village where it turns to mist and is carried away by the wind. Looking around I see I did no damage to anything other than the creature. The wave of relief washes over me. I did not succumb to the darkness.

Walking towards Aiya and Hanako I feel the blood drip from my chin and land on my boots. I expect her to be frightened of me but she looks at me in a way I haven't seen before. It reminds me of the woman I saw with the demon all those years ago. I feel like I am the only person in the world to her.

"Do you want to go in?" asks Hanako.

"No, I want to wait. Just a little longer," says Aiya.

I stand by her closer than I usually do. My demonic nature and the blood on my face doesn't seem to bother her. The three of us stare at the village that is now visible. The fog has evaporated with the centipede. I feel the urge to put my arm around Aiya but there's blood all over me so I resist.

A figure emerges from the village and I see that it's the monk. He rubs his eyes as though he's been asleep. When he sees me his eyes soften and tears beg to spill from them. The monk falls to his knees and gives me a gracious bow meant for the gods. Next emerges a priestess, the one I saw by the shrines the day I brought Aiya here. Her face is tense until she notices me. The creases on her forehead relax and she smiles with her eyes as she bows with the monk. The priestesses behind her do the same.

"Aiya! Aiya!"

"Chiyo!" It's the girl with the widow's peak.

She runs at Aiya fast as lightning and almost knocks her off her feet with an embrace. She shakes as she buries her face in Aiya's neck. Her tears are happy tears. She looks up at me baffled and then looks at

Aiya with understanding. Seeing her up close I notice her eyes are ocean blue and sparkly. She has high cheekbones and defined berry lips. Her hair is black ink that cascades over her shoulders that shake from her crying.

"Aiya, it's him." I am comforted knowing that she never forgot me. That she talked about me even if they didn't believe her. I never stopped thinking about her. She never stopped dreaming about me.

"His name is Riku," says Aiya.

"Thank you, Riku," says the girl with the widow's peak.

She runs off to bow with the others. More and more people come out to greet us. They stare at me and the blood on my face but they all bow. Everyone is bowing to me now. Aiya's friend cheers my name and the others join in.

"Riku! Riku!" they chant.

The monk sits up and gives me a knowing glance before clasping his hands and bowing again. The priestess looks at me like I am a ghost but on her serious face she wears an authentic smile. The crowd keeps growing and they continue cheering my name. Aiya has her hand over her heart as she observes the crowd. As soon as everyone has exited the village she looks up at me with a mix of admiration and wonder.

"You did it, Riku. You saved them," she says.

They chant my name and bow. I hear them clap and sing that I am their savior but it does not touch me the way she does.

"I did it for you."

CHAPTER NINE

The One

I stay to help rebuild the village. Not that I would ever leave Aiya's side now that I've found her. The men and I spend the day resurrecting walls and laying down floors. It takes several of them to transport the lumber necessary but with my assistance we get it done twice as fast. Everyone watches me but I am used to it.

Aiya is sitting with her friend Chiyo at the bottom of the hill. Hanako and Chiyo are similar in the way they do not withhold any affection. They touch her hands, play with her hair, and wrap their arms around her. Being in Aiya's village gives me a glimpse into her life. Brother Minoru and Lady Kiyori are kind and caring people. I can see they have had her best interests at heart.

I'm having a difficult time focusing today. We are repairing Hajime's swordsmith shop. He is the man who gave Aiya that bouquet of lilies all those years ago. He shows me nothing but respect yet I have a gnawing vexation towards him. I hide my irritation by keeping my hands busy and avoiding him as much as possible.

Women come up to Hajime throughout the day and bring him food and water. They touch his arms and laugh at everything he says. He charms them with his handsome smile and clear voice. His jawline is square and strong. He appears consistently at ease. The women come up to me, too. They ask to touch my hair and look into my gold eyes. I don't talk much but when I do they blush and run off. I still don't understand humans.

"Riku, can you help me with this?" asks Hajime.

He gestures towards the wooden boards meant for the shop. I nod my head but don't say anything. The sun is high in the sky and the men are sweaty and tired. The weather has little effect on me, I have fought wars in blizzards and heatwaves. I focus on my work but see Hajime look down the hill at Aiya out of the corner of my eye.

"Aiya is very happy that you're here," he says. He smiles in a thoughtful way that reaches his violet eyes.

"I'm happy she's happy," I say.

"I had a feeling she was waiting for you to come back for her," he announces. I'm surprised but intrigued by his comment.

"What do you mean?"

"I have loved Aiya for a long time. I told her once but she rejected me. I wondered if there was someone else," he says without a hint of jealousy. I stop working to look at him.

"Why would you think it's me?" I ask. My question humors him and he laughs but not in a cruel way.

"You don't see it?" he asks.

"See what?"

"In all the years I've known Aiya I've never seen her look at anyone the way she looks at you," he says.

"I think you're seeing things."

"It's not just the way she looks at you," he says in earnest.

"What is it then?"

"When Aiya sings, she sings about you."

His answer is sincere. He must have heard her song as well. I don't know what to say so I keep my head down and let my bangs fall in my face.

"I'm going to take a break. You should take one, too," he says and goes to sit with the other men.

I lean against the trunk of one of the few oak trees left. It's cooler in the shade but my face is scorching hot.

"Will you be at the celebration tonight?" asks Aiya. I've been lost in my thoughts and didn't hear her walking up the hill.

"Will you be there?"

"Yes," she says. She sounds different this time. She sounds shy.

"Then I will be there," I tell her. Aiya starts walking towards her neighborhood. She looks back at me to wave and smile.

I lean my head back against the bark of the tree and sigh. It's hot but there's a breeze that shakes the leaves from the branches. The wind brings not only the scent of pine needles but something else. There is that aroma of burning rot again. I creep into the forest and walk the perimeter of the village but no sign of Kasai. Unable to relax, I pace around the village half a dozen times.

There are no soot filled foot prints or burnt grass but I know I smell that bitter black blood. I lose track of time and evening is here. In the village the celebration begins but I stand guard. I told Aiya I would be there but feel the need to secure the perimeter again. The scent is gone this time. I survey the forest and see nothing out of the ordinary. I'm not satisfied though. The music gets louder in the village and I hear people cheering. I don't want to miss seeing her and decide to check the perimeter again later.

I stand at the top of the hill and watch the villagers dance and enjoy themselves. Scanning the crowd I see Aiya, she's dancing with Hajime. He knows she loves me yet he still looks at her with tenderness. I commend his ability to care for her without jealousy. The music slows and they notice me watching. He says something to her and lets her go.

"Can I have this dance?" she asks me.

"I'm not one really one to dance."

"Just this once then," she says and grabs the crook of my arm to pull me towards the band.

They all stare at me for a moment, then continue playing another song. Aiya takes my hand and I spin her around. She looks carefree for the first time since I've met her. Hanako and Chiyo dance next to us and they all skip around me. Their kimonos lift with their movements and the silk makes sharp noises as they spin. I haven't felt this way before. Smiling at the thought I realize I feel like I belong. It's getting late, the celebration is ending, but after the music stops Aiya doesn't let go of me.

***

I check the perimeter of the village throughout the night. There is no aroma of burnt decay but I feel a dark energy. In the morning I go to

Aiya's house but she isn't there. It's early in the day and I wonder where she went. I walk around the temple and the shops but I can't find her. Feeling paranoid I pace the perimeter again. As I pass the wisteria trees I pick up the familiar scent of honey and find Aiya sitting by herself plucking at the grass. She looked so happy at the celebration but right now her face is solemn. Aiya blows on her hands and rubs her arms like there's a chill even though it's sunny.

"Are you cold?" I ask and put my cloak over her shoulders.

"Thank you."

"Is something wrong?" I know it's the fire demon.

"It's Kasai. He's coming for me. I know he will be here soon," she says as she pulls another blade of grass.

"I won't let him take you," I assure her.

"You've done so much for me. I don't know how I could ever repay you." Aiya has done more for me than she will ever know.

"You have done enough," I say.

"How?" she asks.

She looks up at me with her deep dark eyes and I can't resist anymore. I embrace her and hold her the way I've wanted to hold her since I first heard her sing about me.

"By being alive," I say.

I expect her to push me away but instead she puts her arms around me and we stay like that until the wisteria trees cast long shadows in the meadow.

***

The aroma of death and fire is potent and I run around the perimeter in search of Kasai. That smell is unmistakable, I know he is close. As I dash through the forest I find the cause of the scent. It's a severed deer head but around it is the black soot footprints. I've been tricked. With a wave of dread I sprint back to the village to look for Aiya. I go to her house but she's not there. I knock on Chiyo's door.

"Hi, Riku. What are you doing?" she asks.

"I'm looking for Aiya. Have you seen her?"

"She said she was going to the hill outside of the village to pick flowers for my brother's wedding," says Chiyo.

I think she wants to say more but I cut her off. The villagers stare at me as I dart past them. I shouldn't have let her out of my sight. Yama's words ring in my ear, "Watch over her, Riku. She is the one."

I can't live with myself if I fail her. If she dies, I die. How could I fall for Kasai's dirty trick? I should have known he was lurking, waiting for the perfect opportunity. I'm leaving the village and the grassy knoll is up ahead. I see her by the treeline picking white flowers and singing to herself. From the shadows of the forest emerges Kasai. The bear head covers most of his face but I can see his disgusting smirk. She looks up and waves at me with a smile that disappears as soon as she sees my expression.

"Aiya!" I call but it's too late.

Kasai surrounds them with his fire barrier. I hit it with my sword but it's useless. The prestigious wolf demon weapon is powerless against him. I have slaughtered armies and killed demons the size of mountains with this blade but it can't help me save the only person that matters. There is nothing I can do. I stand at the fire barrier and call her name. The roar of the flames is deafening but I say her name over and over again.

"Aiya, don't give in to him!"

I can't see what he's doing and I don't know if it would be better or worse to witness. Remembering the way he shoved his serpent tongue in that woman's mouth enrages me and I contemplate using the beast. Even then I don't know if I am capable of stopping Kasai.

"Aiya," I whisper, "I'm right here."

I don't move. All I can do is wait. The crackling of the fire isn't as loud as it was before. Peering through the barrier I see that it is thinning. At first there is just the silhouette of the bear head but as I look closer I can see Aiya. She's leaning into him with one hand on his shoulder and the other at his chest. In her right hand something glows bright white. The barrier continues to recede but I can't get to her. I hear Kasai's sonorous voice echo in the fire.

"No!" he screams.

Aiya has her small knife in his chest and the wound seeps black tar. Soon he is gone and disintegrates into the wind. All that's left is the fur of the bear that he wore.

"Aiya!"

She falls into the grass before I can reach her. Please, don't be dead.

I can't live with myself if she's dead. Once I'm by her side I lift her up and make sure she's breathing. To my relief her chest rises and falls. I grab the knife from her hand to inspect it. The handle is intricately carved and embellished. No doubt Hajime made this for her. My weapon was forged with hellfire, hers was made by someone who loves her.

I'm distracted by the knife and don't notice it at first but once I do my stomach drops. Her hands are adorned with claws like mine and Hanako's. No, this can't be. I part her mouth and see her canines are long and sharp, too. I knew Kasai would violate her but I was not expecting this. My head is spinning and I feel nauseated. I hang my head as I carry her back down the hill. I've failed her. There is no way she'll ever forgive me. Hanako is playing with butterflies outside the village but stops as soon as she sees Aiya in my arms.

"Riku, what happened?"

"It was Kasai," I rasp. Hanako's ears go back and she looks at me and then Aiya. Holding her hand she examines the claws and begins to cry.

"Hanako, please take Aiya." She is reluctant at first but opens her arms. The fox girl looks down and her tears land on Aiya's cheek.

"Poor Aiya..." cries Hanako.

"I have to go," I say and turn to leave.

"Riku, wait! She would want you to be here when she wakes up!"

"No, she won't."

"Please, wait! Come back!" She keeps calling my name but I am in the wind.

CHAPTER TEN

A Blessing and A Curse

Deep in the forest where Aiya won't look for me I find a place to sit down and disappear inside myself. I prop my elbows on my knees and hold my head in my hands staring at the same patch of grass for hours. I never told her how much I love her but it doesn't matter, I'm sure she hates me by now. The ferns and hydrangeas rustle behind me but I don't care to look. I don't care about anything anymore.

"Hey there, pretty boy. Why so glum?" says the tiger demon. In an instant I stand up and grab him by his throat and lift him off the ground.

"Whoa! Down boy!" he laughs.

"What did you do to her?" I ask.

"I don't do anything to anybody that they don't want me to," he says but chokes on his words as I tighten my grip.

"What did you do to her?" I ask again.

"Who? That little mouse you were with? Nothing, I swear!"

"She is not a mouse and I don't believe you," I snarl and look into his sapphire eyes. I despise cat eyes, they are deceitful even if they are telling the truth.

"I didn't touch her. Just ask her!"

"She didn't seem to want to talk about it," I growl at him. I shake him and he yowls.

"Okay, okay. So, maybe I left a little bit out of the story. I propositioned her but she turned me down. I promise I didn't lay a hand on her," he says. I throw him on the ground and put my boot on his chest.

"Don't talk to her. Don't ever talk to her again."

"Yes, your majesty."

His comment infuriates me and I kick him in the side. He cries out in pain and it feels so good to hurt something. He brushes himself off and for once he's not swishing that damn tail around.

"Now get out of my sight!" I bark. He puts his hands up and backs away, then retreats into the shadows of the trees.

I go back to feeling sorry for myself and bury my face in my knees. As I try and hide inside myself I wonder if the gods laugh or cry for me. Something is messing with my hair and I push it away but don't bother to acknowledge what it is. A small snout keeps ruffling up the hair on the top of my head and I shoo it away. It doesn't stop though.

"What do you want?" I snap and look up to see the white deer. She stares at me with those otherworldly eyes.

"Leave me alone," I sigh.

She tries to mess with my hair again and I use my foot to push her away. Every time I put my leg down she attempts to get close to me but I extend my arm and keep her at a distance. The deer won't leave me be.

"I already know I failed so just go away." She backs up startled but her eyes bore holes into my soul. The deer decides to lay down in front of me.

"I don't even know what you want! Find someone else," I bark at her.

"Is that any way to talk to the gods' messenger?" says a familiar voice. I look over my shoulder to see Satoru.

"I don't know why she keeps bothering me. I have failed," I say. Satoru sits next to the white deer and they gaze into each other's eyes for a moment.

"She says you didn't fail."

"You can understand her?"

"I can't send a message but I can understand them," he replies.

"What else is she saying?"

"She says that things are exactly as they should be."

"Exactly as they should be? The woman I love, the person I swore to protect, has been defiled by Kasai. Even in death he lives on inside her." As I say this my heart breaks and I can't keep in the tears I've been fighting since I saw Aiya in the fire barrier.

"The gods knew Aiya was the one," says Satoru. I remember Yama's howl that I didn't understand, "Watch over her, Riku. She is the one."

"What do you mean?"

"The gods knew Aiya would have the power to kill Kasai. But she wouldn't have been able to do it without your help," says Satoru through his strange mouth.

"I wasn't much help to her," I say.

"You saved Aiya that day Kasai came to collect her. Because she lived on she was loved, and because she was loved she was able to break her own curse and defeat him."

"Now she's cursed to live the rest of her life as a demon," I spit. This makes Satoru chuckle and the white deer twitches her ears and looks at me again.

"What's so funny?" I ask.

"Aiya is not cursed. Just because Kasai changed her doesn't mean she is not herself. You are able to walk the sacred grounds of Aiya's village because your heart is pure, too."

I never thought about that. Yama said I would carry something precious onto sacred grounds. At the time I didn't worry about the ground burning and purifying me as I had been taught. I only cared about her safety.

"You should go to her. She needs you," says Satoru.

"I doubt that."

"Aiya is one of us now. She needs someone to guide her and show her our world."

"The white deer should find someone better suited for the task," I say.

She gets up and stands close enough to my face that I can feel her short, rapid breaths. The demigod comes to my other side and looks at her while speaking into my ear.

"Aiya has been waiting for you to come back for her since the day you rescued her. Even when no one believed a demon would save a human, she believed in you. She has always loved you, Riku. There is no one else to her," says Satoru.

"I just want her to be happy," I say.

"You should be happy. Now she will live for centuries and you will never be alone again," says Satoru and as he does the white deer bounds away.

***

I race back to the village feeling foolish for abandoning her when she needs me the most. By the time I get there it's dark. I'm worried when I get to Aiya's house and see she's not there. Maybe she's at Chiyo's.

"Hi, Riku. What's going on?"

"I'm looking for Aiya," I say. Her face changes and I can tell that something's wrong.

"She was really scared when she woke up. I tried to call for her to come back but she ran away. I'm sorry, Riku. I don't know where she went," she says.

Chiyo is a joyful person like Hanako but right now her demeanor is melancholy. I chide myself for being selfish and running off.

"It's okay, Chiyo. I'll find her," I assure her. I know Chiyo is important to Aiya, so she is important to me. I search the whole village but no sign or scent of her. Running the perimeter is fruitless as well. Just to be sure I do another lap.

"Riku!" It's Hanako.

"Have you seen Aiya?" I ask.

"No. I'm looking for her, too."

"I feel awful about leaving the way I did," I admit. The fox girl puts her hand on my shoulder and smiles.

"I know you were scared. I was, too."

"It's more than that," I say. This surprises Hanako. I haven't opened up to her about how I feel but I know she is clever and she saw me cry that night before we reached Aiya's village.

"You can tell me, Riku. I'm your friend."

"What if Aiya doesn't forgive me?"

"Aiya doesn't blame you for what Kasai did to her," says Hanako.

"I blame myself. I should have known he was watching her," I say.

The fox girl hugs me and rubs my back to try and make me feel better.

"I messed up, too. Kasai found us in the forest and I knew he planned to take her right then. I used the bird feathers I picked up that morning to glide across the cliff to get her away from him. After we landed I had to make the decision to protect Aiya the only way I could and I left her all alone in the forest," she cries.

I would have never guessed Hanako felt like she had failed Aiya.

"That's when I found her," I whisper.

***

Hanako and I look for Aiya all night but she is in the wind. Feeling anxious and remorseful I head to the temple. I want to see the sacred grounds. The sun isn't up yet and there are no priestesses at the shrines or the basins. There's a creek lined with cherry blossom trees. It leads me to the sacred spring where I left Aiya. The dirt hasn't burned me but I am curious about the water. I kneel to stick my hand in the holy liquid expecting pain but feel nothing except the slight stir of the spring.

"Riku?" The monk appears. Embarrassed, I snatch my hand back and look down.

"You may be a demon but you have a pure heart. Your blood runs red like ours," he says in a gentle tone.

"I am lost," I admit.

"What do you mean?" he asks as he sits down, clasping his hands in a pious way that reminds me of Yama.

"All my life I was told humans and demons live in different worlds. We have different ways, different laws. But after I left my home in the northern mountains I've seen things that amaze and confuse me," I say.

The monk grins at me, closing his eyes before speaking.

"As have I. The day you brought Aiya to us I saw you walk through the sacred grounds. I remember wondering how you could do that but after you set her down I knew," he says. There are deep creases around his eyes from his smile.

"Knew what?" I ask.

"That our worlds are not so far apart."

"Have you ever seen a half demon?" I ask. He raises his eyebrows at my question.

"No," he says and shakes his head.

"I did once. At first I thought something was wrong. Then I got closer and saw that they were a family. The woman and the demon she was with looked at their baby with such affection. It has been on my mind for many years," I say. This pleases the monk and he covers his heart with his hand.

"Love is the strongest force in the world."

***

I go back to the hill where Kasai changed Aiya and find her on her knees touching the burnt grass and dead flowers. She clutches her heart as though it will give her the answers that she seeks.

"Aiya," I say her name through the lump in my throat.

"Riku, I was just looking for you." She looks at me with the same red eyes Kasai had.

"I'm sorry. I feel like I failed you," I admit.

"You have never failed me," she says.

I take her hand and examine her claws that match mine. My gain isn't her curse and the ache in my chest subsides. My sword is seeped in the demonic energy of the water dragon. I thought it was meant only to bring fortune for war but maybe it has brought me luck in an unexpected way.

"What happened to you in the fire barrier?" I ask.

"Kasai tried to rip out my heart and erase my memories. I stabbed him in the chest with this," she says and shows me the knife that Hajime made her.

"How did you defeat him?" I ask.

"He tried to make me forget my baby brother, Takara. It didn't work though. I'll always remember him. Even if I forget myself."

We turn to the sun that tints the sky pink and orange. I see her watching it with a new perspective. Even though she doesn't move her mouth I can see the smile in her eyes. The sky turns blue and I do something I regret not doing the day I saw tears in her lash line as she sang about me. I kiss her and she kisses me back.

"I never want to lose you," I say.

"You won't. I'm like you now. I'm strong," she says. I can't help but admire the strength that she's had this whole time.

"You've always been strong. Even when you were human."

***

I thought Aiya would want to stay near the village where her friends and family are but she makes the decision to leave with me. We wait until after Chiyo's brother's wedding. The ceremony is decorated with white camellias and red spider lilies. A river of red and white flowers lines the village and everyone watches how Yuta never lets go of his new bride.

Aiya stays by my side everywhere I go. She holds my hand when we walk and we sleep in each other's arms. I rest my head in her lap and she runs her fingers through my hair as she sings to me.

It's you, it's you
Who left me by the spring
The man that I love
The reason why I sing
We were far apart
But fate brought you back to me

Her frown is gone and she smiles all the time. The darkness may have touched her but it made the light in her glow brighter. Aiya and I dance with her friends and they treat me as one of them.

"I wish you both happiness," says Hajime as he gives me a small bow.

He thinks I saved Aiya, but it is his love, and the love Aiya has for her baby brother that was the catalyst. Their own magic had the power to defeat the fire demon.

"Thank you, Hajime," I say, "your gift kept Aiya alive," I add. Hajime straightens up at my words but shows no sign of arrogance.

"Be safe out there," he says as he goes back to the celebration.

"Are you ready?" I ask her.

She nods at me and we head up the hill where the white flowers grow. We turn around to watch the village from the top and marvel at it together.

"I'm glad you chose this place," she sighs.

"You are?" I ask.

"Yes. I had a wonderful life there."

"Will you be happy now?" I know she will say "yes" but I need her to reassure me and she does.

"I'm about to live the most extraordinary life," she answers. The wind picks up her long hair and kimono. She throws her head back and opens her arms to the breeze.

"Wait for me!" shouts Hanako as she bounds through the tall grass to meet us.

The fox girl has shown me that to be strong is to be kind. That not all power lies within force or draws blood. To be able to make magic where there is none is a talent of hers. I will forever be indebted to the fox princess for protecting Aiya. She disagrees though, she says she would do anything for me because I am her friend.

"Where do you want to go?" I ask Aiya.

"Take me to the place where we first met. I know nothing from my old life will be there but I need to see it one last time," she says.

"As you wish."

With her new abilities we are able to transcend the spectral plain and the spirits of the forest no longer hide from us. They line our path as we race through the woods faster than the river where the water dragon lives. There will be obstacles and struggles but we will have each other. Aiya is part of my world now. I have so much to teach her but thinking about all of the time we will have together comforts me.

Aiya will live for centuries. She doesn't need me to protect her anymore but I will. She is my summer in the harshest winter. I remember staring at the constellation Gemini the year I left home and longing to be closer to it. The girl with stars on her face has been loved by many but I am the one who will love her forever.

PART TWO

My Name is Aiya

CHAPTER ELEVEN

Turned to Ash

Our home collapses and sparks fly. The roof of the neighboring house is on fire. Smoke envelops the village in a thick black fog. I can't find my parents. Everyone is running this way and that. We are all looking for someone, shouting their names. I'm calling for my mother and father, saying my sister's name, and whispering my little brother's. Where are they? The dirt is packed and warm from a hundred panicked feet. I try to ask someone for help.

"Have you seen my father?" They look at each other before shaking their heads "no" and scurrying away like frightened mice. Everything is on fire now. All the shops, the fields of rice, and our homes. People riding horseback pass me with large bundles. They attempt to flee but a burning tree falls in front of them cutting off their path. Spooked, the horses buck and take off in all directions.

The sleeves of my kimono are burnt and frayed, turning the once pink fabric dark brown. My hands are covered in ash and my eyes burn. I have to find my parents. I need to know if my little brother and sister are okay. Families pass me carrying their children and baskets filled to the brim.

"Excuse me, have you seen my mother or father?" I ask. My voice is breathless. I'm growing desperate.

"No, I'm sorry."

"Thank you," I say.

"Aiya," it's one of the women carrying a baby. "Be careful."

I nod my head before I turn and run into the dark. More terrified faces go by in a blur but none of them are the faces I need to see. It starts to rain but I can't feel it on my skin. My hands and feet are numb. I hear screams. So many people scream in succession. Men, women, and children call out in agony.

"Help us!"

"What is it?"

"Please, no–" their voices blend into one another but the message is clear: there is something in the village.

Despite the rain the fire begins to grow around us. A wall of flames traps everyone inside. I can hear flesh and muscle being sliced through. The smell of blood mixes with the smoke and mud. I hide behind what's left of a destroyed home and listen to the voices of my people.

"Get away from me!"

"Stop!"

"Why are you doing this?"

I make slow movements to peek around the corner and get a glimpse of the intruder. I can't see him but I can make out his shadow. Beyond the burning buildings I see him tear out someone's rib cage and shred another person apart. I can't differentiate the crackle and pop of ripping sinew from the sounds of the fire. I can hear his boots shatter bone and wet screams. Blood can be distinguished from the rain as it hits the ground.

His shape is that of a person but this was no human. Our village is run by several powerful monks and priestesses. We have been fortunate to not have as many problems with demons as others. I cover my mouth to conceal my gasp. Unable to watch the slaughter I lean against the wall with my knees to my chest and my palms pressed over my ears. The cries could not be drowned out. My body trembles with fear. I look to my left and I see his shadow approaching. Without thinking I shoot up and run. My mind is blank but my body carries me swiftly without orders.

Then I see them, bodies, more than twenty. Severed heads with lifeless stares. Limbs are strewn about the ground, some of them still writhing. No one runs past me. There isn't anyone left standing. A child's arm holding a small toy brings up bitter bile in my throat.

"Father!" I cry. His body is split at the torso. With the last of his strength he reaches out to me.

"Aiya," his voice is shaky.

"Father, please. Don't leave me," I say through my tears and touch his hand to my cheek.

"I love you, Aiya. I'm so...I'm so sorry," he says before his arm goes limp.

"No! Father, please. Please come back to me."

It was a childish plea. It's pointless to call for him but I do. The demon following me is closing in but I don't move. I want to be with my family. I close my eyes and wait for death. The silence is deafening. I feel arms around my waist and I know my time has come. My father's hand slips from mine as he grabs me.

"We have to go," says a man I have never seen before.

He has white hair and amber eyes. Before I can protest he picks me up and begins to run with inhuman speed. Over his shoulder I see the shadow of the demon who terrorized the village.

"Who are you?" I ask.

"No one," he replies. All the trees are going by too fast. It's making me dizzy. I feel myself fading but before I let go I take one more look at him. I want to remember his face.

Then I wake up. I have this dream often. Even though it's been almost six years I still remember the touch of my dying father and the face of the man who saved me.

The day after my home was destroyed I woke up in this village led by Brother Minoru and Lady Kiyori. They have cared for me since my strange arrival. I was found near the sacred spring. Their worried faces hovered over me as they spoke in hushed tones. I didn't talk for three days.

They questioned what happened to me and I blurted out that someone set my village on fire and that a demon brought me here. This caused their faces to contort. Their reaction brought me great shame. I knew they didn't believe me. No one did, but they accepted me into their community so I'm indebted to them.

I'm running late for my duties and I rush through the morning routine. I throw on my favorite blue and red kimono. The yellow obi is smooth and shiny. I comb my long black hair before putting half of it up and pinning it with the hair sticks my mother gave me, the only things I have left from my old life.

They have red spider lilies on them. Our favorite flower. We used to sit in the meadow where they grew and when the wind blew it looked like scarlet waves. My sister Emi was a year younger than me. Her favorite color was purple and she loved irises. Takara, my baby brother, was fond of every flower.

I finish washing up and slip on my sandals. I step out of the small house and shield my eyes from the bright day and blink to adjust to the morning light. My neighbor and best friend Chiyo is about to leave her house as well. She gives me a smile and waves me over.

"Aiya! Are you on your way to Brother Minoru and Lady Kiyori?"

"Yes, another busy day."

"Let's walk together," she says in a cheery tone and locks her elbow with mine.

"Where are you off to?" I ask.

"To do all the stuff my brother refuses to do, of course!" she says and we both laugh.

Yuta's disdain for stopping by the shops and waiting in line for rice was amusing. He would tend to the horses and fish in the river but asking him to pick up something from the apothecary was offensive.

Chiyo and Yuta have the same widow's peak and high cheekbones. Their eyebrows are thick and shapely. She has pretty strawberry lips. They both have deep blue eyes that remind me of stormy evenings. Chiyo is very playful whereas it's rare to see Yuta wear a smile. After I arrived in the village no one would speak to me except Lady Kiyori and Brother Minoru. One day Chiyo came up to me with a rice ball and said "here, let's be friends."

It took time but eventually everyone else warmed up to me. I think her inviting nature made others more comfortable in my presence. One thing I learned early on was to not talk about the demon who rescued me. Even Chiyo doesn't believe my story. Both her and Lady Kiyori say that the mind can play tricks on us. I had been through a terrible thing and it has become distorted in my memory.

As we walk through the village we smile at the shopkeepers sweeping their entry places. Two young men pull carts carrying melons and bok choy. Chiyo and I wave in passing and they turn bright red as they stutter "good morning." On our way to the market we see our friends carrying baskets of clothes.

"Good morning!" Chiyo exclaims.

"Chiyo, Aiya! Good morning," says Natsume.

"Where are you off to?" Chiyo asks the group.

"To the river to wash our clothes. My husband's kimono smells so bad I might just throw it in and say I lost it," teases Daina as she holds her nose.

"Not as bad as my husband's! It's worse than rotting fish," jokes Hiromi as she fans her basket. The other ladies laugh and so do we.

"Just wait until you have your own husband's dirty laundry," says Natsume with her basket balanced on her hip.

"I can't wait to be married," says Chiyo with her hands clasped.

Her dreamy expression annoys me but I don't say anything. I'm not interested in marriage or children. After all I had lost I could not bear losing another precious thing.

"Aiya, I hear the swordsmith's son has his eyes on you," says Daina. She gives me a sly grin.

"He is a respectable man. Works hard and is very kind. You should consider," Hiromi tells me.

I know they mean well but I don't have those feelings for Hajime. We only see each other at his family's shop. Their craft is spectacular and I enjoy admiring the blades more as works of art than weapons. I am impressed by the dedication they put into every piece, each one unique to the owner.

Priests, priestesses, and samurais came from all over to have Tetsuma make them a sword. Hajime's father knew I fancied their work and he would beckon me inside every time I walked past. He would say he had something to show me and I would be forced to wait in the shop alone with Hajime.

"Thank you. But I am not sure he is interested in me," I reply, trying to be polite.

"I've seen the way his face lights up when he sees you. That's a man in love if I've ever seen one," says Hiromi.

"He is one of the most handsome men in the village, Aiya! I can't believe you're not jumping at the chance," chimes Natsume. I don't know how to respond. I didn't know Hajime's affection was this obvious to everyone.

"I suppose we'll see," I say as I gesture to leave.

"Good bye! Good bye!" they call to us as we part ways.

We walk most of the way in silence. I am lost in thought about my recurring dream. I don't know if he's real but I think about him all the time. Chiyo stops me and takes my hand.

"Aiya, why don't you marry Hajime?" she asks with sad eyes. Not her usual expression.

"I don't know, Chiyo. I haven't really thought about marriage to anybody," I reply. Taking a step back I break from her grasp. It's honest enough but I don't want to explain myself further.

"I wish someone wanted to marry me," moans Chiyo as she drags her feet behind me.

"I'm sure someone does. You'll be married in no time so don't worry, okay?"

"Okay," she says in an exasperated tone, "I'm going to take care of my errands. See you later."

"Bye, Chiyo! I'll see you at home." I'm glad to be by myself the rest of the walk. It gives me time to collect my thoughts. I arrive at the sacred grounds and Brother Minoru is waiting for me.

"Good morning, Aiya."

"Good morning, Brother Minoru."

"Shall we?"

"Yes," I say and he guides me to the garden with the shrines.

"If you could pull the weeds from the flower beds and rake the leaves by the shrines today," says Brother Minoru in his gentle voice.

"Of course. Anything else, Brother Minoru?" I ask as I roll up the sleeves of my kimono.

"That will be all today. Thank you, Aiya. Be well," he says as he exits the garden.

I don't mind working at the sacred grounds. Sometimes I work here in the garden or I sweep the temple and wash the floors. Lady Kiyori has me scrub the basins used for holy water and prepare the herbs meant to repel demons. It's tedious work but keeping my hands busy soothes my racing mind.

I can't stop thinking about what the women said about Hajime. Am I really so ridiculous? They were saying I should consider myself lucky since I'm the crazy girl who claims a demon brought her here.

Hajime was handsome, strong, and kind. A respected member of the community. Still, I did not have those feelings for him. Brushing the beads of sweat from my brow I continue to pull at the weeds as if extracting thoughts.

Chiyo and I are so different. She longs for a man to fall in love with her. Most of her shooting star wishes are to be married and have a child. Warm and bright like the sunrise. A singsong voice that is as light as the sky. Anytime someone is sad she is the one who cheers them up. She is the first to give you her lunch or pick a flower and put it in your hair. Always a sympathetic touch before she says everything will be okay. Forever in my heart, my sweet best friend.

My voice isn't silvery or high like most young women my age, it's low and husky. It doesn't matter though, I don't talk much. I have difficulties making pleasantries with acquaintances. It doesn't come naturally to me the way it does for Chiyo. Earlier today was mortifying. They act in jest but I felt completely uncomfortable. How they could be open about their husband's stinking laundry and point out Hajime's affection is beyond me. Even though it's been years I'm still very formal with most of the community. It's not my intention to be standoffish but I remember the way they would whisper about me. Their eyes fixated on me as they leaned to one another. Soon after Chiyo initiated our friendship she asked me what everyone was wondering.

"Aiya, where did you come from? How did you get here?" she asked in her high voice. I was still in a daze at the time. Fearful, fatherless, and forsaken.

"A man came to my village and set everything on fire," I started. Chiyo urged me to go on.

"I saw their bodies on the ground. Dozens of them. The man was not really a man. He came for me," I continued. Chiyo's dark blue eyes were large and glossy as she studied my face.

"What happened next?" she asked after I paused for a long time.

"He saved me," I trailed off.

"The man who burned down the village?" Chiyo was confused.

"No. There was another man. He had these gold eyes. He was carrying me. Then I woke up here," I finished.

"Are you sure it wasn't just a dream?" she asked in earnest.

"I'm not sure. Maybe it was," I said, not wanting to talk about the subject anymore.

"It's okay, Aiya. You're safe here. I'll protect you forever," she said.

Then she hugged me and played with my hair. I cried silent tears as she held me tighter. I put my arms around her and knew she would be precious to me regardless of how different we were.

I'm done with the weeds and I begin raking the leaves that fall from the camphor trees. Stepping on small twigs releases an invigorating scent. Breathing it in I feel a sense of calm as I carry out the rest of my duties while I sing.

Was it you, was it you
Who hid me in the tree
Covered me in leaves
There was a man
I know he came for me
The smoke hides his face
Even in my dreams
Who was he, who was he

The birds call to me and I call back. Their songs keep me company during my work. I don't care for the constant companionship of people but animals had a way of making me feel safe but not smothered. Hearing the flutter of wings and the melodies they produced were enough.

It's time to do my rounds and check on all the flower beds to be sure I didn't miss a weed. It fills me with pride to see that I have done a thorough job. The grass is clear of pine cones, acorns, and other debris. The shrines are free of dust and dirt. I turn to admire the sacred grounds. It feels good to make something beautiful.

I sit in the shade under an oak to take a break. To entertain myself I make shapes out of the clouds that pass by. First there was one that had the likeness of a horse. Another appears in the shape of a dragon. I wish life could be creamy and soft as a cloud. Instead it's metal and rock. Life does not bend with the breeze. I sit up and lean against the sturdy trunk. It's almost time to go home. I note the texture of the bark and stare at its roots. They are strong and grounded. For years I have felt like I am floating in the wind, a specter without a body. To see the tree strong and planted made me yearn to have an anchor within myself.

I search for Brother Minoru to see if I am needed anywhere else on the grounds today. There are three priestesses near the temple but no sign of Lady Kiyori. Behind the temple is a small creek. I follow it for a while before I find Brother Minoru. He appears to be deep in thought standing beneath the cherry blossom trees.

"Brother Minoru, I apologize if I am disturbing you," I say as I get closer. His mouth is tense and his brows are furrowed but he brightens as soon as he sees me.

"Not all, Aiya. What is it?"

"May I go? I have finished my duties for the day."

"Of course. Have a good night. I will see you tomorrow." He winces as though he's in pain.

"Good night. I'll see you tomorrow," I tell him. Before I get too far I turn back to see the grave look on his face again.

"Brother Minoru?"

"Yes?"

"Do you know where Lady Kiyori is? I haven't seen her all day," I ask over my shoulder.

"I believe she had some business to tend to in a neighboring village," he replies without looking at me.

Something feels off but I ignore it and head home. By the time I reach my house the sun is setting and I'm starving.

"Aiya!" Chiyo runs over to me holding a skewered fish and a pear.

"How did you know?" I laugh as I take a large bite.

"A best friend has a way of knowing these things," she teases.

"How was your day, Chiyo?"

"It was alright. Yuta is driving me crazy though," she rolls her eyes.

"What's he doing now?"

"That's the thing! He's doing nothing at all! I try to get him to hang out with us and he declines to sit around and sulk."

"That's Yuta for you. Always in a sour mood." I half smile.

"You're one to talk!"

"I'm not sour! I'm just thinking a lot is all," I argue.

"I wonder what Yuta's thinking about."

"Have you asked him?"

"Yes! And you know what he says? 'Nothing,'" she draws out the word in a glum voice mocking her brother.

"Hey, give him a break. When he's ready he'll come around," I assure her.

"I hope so. Well, I better get going. I'll come get you in the morning so we can walk together. Goodnight, Aiya!"

"Goodnight, Chiyo. Thank you for dinner. You're the best."

"I'm the best and you're blessed," she sings as she skips to her house.

"Yeah, I guess I really am," I say to myself.

CHAPTER TWELVE

Faith

Today is my nineteenth birthday. It's also the anniversary of the day my village was decimated. I see his face in my dreams again. The tousled white hair waving in the wind against the night sky. Intense amber eyes would haunt me forever. I wonder why I wake up and I miss him. He was just a ghost.

My thirteenth birthday…it's hard to look back at that day. To see the little girl in the pink kimono running scared through the village to find her dying her father tormented my soul. I am most melancholy on my birthday. They were once a welcomed holiday. Now they serve as an ugly reminder of who I used to be.

I still appear the same but I'm a couple inches taller. Ink black hair and dark eyes. My face resembles my mother's now. The shape of her chin, small nose, and thin smile belong to me now. I was the only one in our family with freckles and they splash across my face in the shape of the constellation Gemini. Emi used to connect them from under my left eye, across the bridge of my nose, and to my cheek.

"This is us," she would whisper, "two sisters, one soul." The sound of her voice is fresh in my mind. I try to shake away the skeletons of my past life as I wash my face and get ready for the day. It's time to go to the market and pick up the necessities. I go outside and see Yuta leaning in the doorway. I wave to him and he gives me an apathetic wave back but no sign of Chiyo in the neighborhood. She must have had some errands to do as well. On my way I run into

Hiromi and Daina.

"Happy birthday, Aiya!" they say with cheer as we near each other.

"Thank you. How are you two today?" I ask but I'm not really interested.

My birthday is bittersweet around the village. They try to make it a happy day but it just isn't. I can't be angry with them for trying though.

"Not so bad! Looking for Natsume, have you seen her?" asks Hiromi.

"No, I haven't. Sorry," I reply.

"It's okay, we'll find her. More of a reason to stay out of the house!" says Daina, which causes the two of them to break into a fit of laughter.

"Good luck with your search," I say. As I walk past them I can feel their eyes on me.

"Bye, Aiya! Have a good day," I hear them call but I don't turn around.

There are a couple other people examining the baskets of vegetables and rice by the time I get to the market. No one is looking at each other and we shop without formalities. This is what I wanted, to blend in, and not be noticed.

Since it's my birthday I browse around a bit longer looking at the high quality inks and parchment paper. I run my hands along several types of silk. There are powders made of jasmine, star anise, cloves, and cinnamon. I enjoy the fragrant oils made of roses, sweet almonds, and oranges.

They all smell incredible but I pick the floral and citrus one. The woman selling them gives me a sympathetic look and says I can have it for free. I protest but she shoves it in my hands and tells me to take it. After spending the afternoon shopping I realize how hungry I am. I still have coins left so I search for one of the vendors that makes fried fish or eel around this time. On a normal day I would just eat one of the turnips or apples in my basket but I feel sullen and wasteful.

The greasy eel tastes much more satisfying than one of the root vegetables I bought. I don't regret my decision. The priestesses walk through the village and they bow to me in passing. They wear red trousers and tie up their hair with paper ribbons. One of the girls is a few years younger than me. She has a bow and arrows while the others carry swords. We make eye contact the entire time and I feel like she is attempting to see into my soul. Still no sign of Lady Kiyori.

Before I head home I stop by the swordsmith's shop. I allowed Natsume, Hiromi, and Daina's conversation to embarrass me and it kept me from feeling comfortable talking to Hajime. Upon entering the shop I see his father.

"Aiya! Happy birthday! Wait right there. Let me get Hajime," says Tetsuma through his long beard.

"That isn't necessary–" I say but he cuts me off and walks to the back of the shop.

The clanking of metal in the back room stops. A moment later Hajime is standing before me. His hairline is damp with sweat from using the hammer and folding steel. With his defined jawline and plum colored eyes he is pleasing to look at.

Hajime has short hair that he wears down unlike most men in the village who wear it up. He hands me a present. Wrapped in a deep blue cloth is a small knife that glistens in the sun. The handle is intricately carved and embellished.

"I made this with special properties. It will keep you safe," he says as he holds my hands in his for a moment.

They're twice the size of mine and strong. Gentle but rough from his labor intensive days. His arms are muscular from working with metal all day. I wish his smile would wake something inside me but all I feel is emptiness.

"Oh, Hajime. Thank you, but you don't have to give me anything."

"Please, take it. It would bring me happiness for you to have it." His mouth is curved into a thoughtful smile. What's wrong with me? Hiromi and Daina would die to be in Hajime's arms but here I am trying to slip from his grasp like a slippery fish. I pull up the corners of my lips and try to give him a warm look.

"It's wonderful. Thank you."

"Happy birthday, Aiya."

"I'm nineteen now," I blurt out more for myself than him.

"Yes. I remember the first time I saw you many years ago." His gaze is dreamy and my face is becoming hot.

"What do you remember?"

"A beautiful girl fell from the sky and into my life."

"Hajime, I'm flattered. I'm sorry, I don't know what to say."

"It's okay, you don't have to say anything. I know you have been through a lot. Just know that you mean so much to me. I hope maybe someday you will find your feelings for me," he says as he lets go of my hands.

"Have a good night."

"Good night," he's barely finished his sentence as I exit from the shop and turn down the path to my house.

Once I'm out of sight I cover my face with the sleeve of my kimono and let out a sob. I dry the tears from my eyes as I near the neighborhood. The basket is filled to the brim with vegetables, the floral oil, and a portion of rice but I don't feel satisfied anymore.

The joy of getting all the items I wanted has worn off. The sun is low in the sky but hasn't set yet. Orange and purple clouds line the horizon. The distant mountains to the north are slate and indigo peaks. I stare at them as I walk.

The quiet is making me uneasy. No one is sweeping their stoop or tending to their herb garden. Children often play by the pond with the koi fish but the water is still and there is no sound of laughter or running feet. I'm becoming worried. Where is everyone? My chest is tight and I am on high alert. I tread with soft steps up to my house. My breathing is shallow and my fingers ache from gripping the basket. Please no, not again…

"Surprise!" Chiyo, Yuta, Natsume, Hiromi, and Daina jump out at me. I'm relieved, this is where everyone was. They are having a party for me.

"Happy birthday, Aiya!" Chiyo squeezes me and I feel as though I may faint.

"Thanks, Chiyo," I rasp.

"Here, have some mussels! My husband got them this morning and I prepared them with a spicy sauce for you," says Natsume. She holds out a ginormous pot of delicious seafood to me.

"This is great! Thank you." I'm genuine with my thanks as I pull the mussel from its shell with my teeth. It's hot and burns my lips but tastes so good I have another right away.

"Try one of my salmon rice balls, Aiya!" Hiromi is holding a tray of spectacular fare.

"Yes, of course! Thank you." Before I can say anything more she shoves a bite of seaweed and salmon in my mouth. It's salty but flavorful.

"Save room for dessert," Daina and the neighbors hold large bowls of diced fruits with red bean paste and honey.

"You are all too kind. Thank you. You didn't have to go through so much trouble." I am beginning to feel shy. Everyone's trying to make me feel special.

"Happy birthday, Aiya. Hey, are you going to eat that?" says Yuta as he eyes the last rice ball.

"Here, I'm stuffed. You have it," I say. He accepts and runs off with his prize.

"Wait! There's more!" exclaims Chiyo.

"More? How could I possibly need anything else?"

"Every woman needs something pretty. That's what my mom used to say," she places something on my wrist. It's a thin gold bracelet.

"Oh, Chiyo. I can't accept this," I say in awe of my friend's generosity.

"We all went in on it. You're a part of our family, Aiya. I know you don't always think so but you are. I want this bracelet to remind you. Look closely at it," she says as her eyes sparkle.

I take off the bracelet and upon further inspection I see the engraving. It read "cherished." I cover my mouth to keep from having too many emotions spill out at once.

"Thank you everyone. I appreciate all the time and effort you put into making my birthday special. I'm so touched." I feel my voice start to shake and I stop there. Nothing else needed to be said.

***

I wake up and reach for the empty side of my bed. Why? I dream about him again. A starry night is dull compared to the man with white hair and gold eyes. I can handle witnessing my father die and the shadow of the demon as long as I see him. Sitting up I feel heavy with grief. It sits in my lower back and pulls on the strings attached to my heart.

To start the day I wash my face and brush the inky locks. I put my hair up and tie it with a ribbon. I adorn it with the hair sticks. Examining myself longer than most days I notice the freckles on my face seem darker than usual. I clean my teeth and put on my yellow kimono with the green obi. This one makes me feel pretty on sunny days.

Stepping outside I see the neighbors tend to daily chores. Sweeping their homes, pulling weeds from gardens, and hanging clothes out on the line to dry. I take my clothes to the river to wash. Chiyo isn't home so I go alone. I find solace in my own company most of the time. My kimonos are shades of red, yellow, and blue. Chiyo wears hues of pink and green. I am a fire or a storm. A heatwave and a bottomless sea. My best friend is a welcoming field of flowers. She is my hideaway. An escape from the harshness of reality. Her voice is the ringing of a bell that calls me home.

The path to the river is lined with baby roses and ferns. The day is new and everything is coated with sunshine. I look up and let the yellow orb kiss my face. Closing my eyes it feels like the gods are casting their light in my direction. I open them and watch orange butterflies flutter over the boulders. They play hide and seek.

I miss my mother. We would chase butterflies and sing to the birds. I saw her pet a red deer once. He was captivated by her and allowed her to approach him. She was a wonderful person. Everyone loved her. Men fell at her feet but she saw only my father. My mother sang to the birds so often that they refused to sing until she sang first. I remember waiting outside for the sunrise as a child. Even after the sun was up they remained silent until she came out and called to them.

As I wash my clothes I feel like I am being watched. I look over my shoulder. There is no one. I stand up and squint to see across the river. Nobody is standing at the treeline. I kneel back down and continue to scrub the red kimono with blue floral designs. My favorite one. A branch breaks off a tree and makes me jump.

"Hello?" I call to the forest. "Is somebody there?"

No one answers me and I feel disappointed. To drown out the sadness I wring out silk until my hands are raw and my wrists hurt.

Feeling satisfied that all my clothes are clean I get up to leave. I pause and watch the wind blow through the tall grass outside the dark woods. Leaves sway and make crinkling paper noises. A robin lands on a branch in front of me. It looks at me like he has something to tell me.

"Who's there?" I ask the shadows.

Waiting for a reply makes me tense. I bounce the basket on my hip and look around. There's no way it's him but what if it is? I step closer to the forest but stop at the ferns. Another step leads me into the darkness. I scold myself for being afraid and walk along the river.

Silver fish shimmer under the surface. The water is loud but it helps me rid myself of these pesky thoughts. I wonder if he ever came back for me. Then I feel foolish. He is an apparition. Just a dream. There's another creaking sound amongst the trees. I look into the oaks and camphors. The hydrangeas tint the green and black forest with hues of blue.

"Hello?" I call again. I am met with nothing but the rustling leaves. The smell of camphor is potent here. Its medicinal scent makes my nose twitch.

"Goodbye," I say to no one as I walk the path back to the village.

***

My bracelet shimmers in the early morning sun. I'm raking the stray leaves and pine cones from the sacred grounds. Ever since my birthday I have felt something stirring in me. I was overwhelmed by everyone's contribution. I never felt close to anybody here except Chiyo. It's difficult to imagine others caring about me in such a deep way. Now I try harder to converse with Natsume, Hiromi, and Daina.

I always thought they were Chiyo's friends, not mine. The smile on Natsume's face as she handed me the bowl of seafood was not out of obligation but out of true joy. Hiromi expressed such excitement when I praised the salmon rice balls. Daina and the neighbors displayed their dishes with authentic enthusiasm. They really did care. Maybe not in the ways I would prefer but everyone has different ways of showing their affection.

I haven't gone to Tetsuma's shop for two weeks now. Hajime is sweet but I don't long for him the way a wife should. It's better not to get his hopes up so I avoid that area of the village. I don't dare tell Chiyo about what he said. She would chide me on how ungrateful I'm being. It's true, I am guilty of that. The word "cherished" echoes in my mind and reminds me to appreciate others.

Lady Kiyori has been back for a while but we haven't spoken. She seems distracted. Brother Minoru as well. The priestesses have been walking around with solemn faces. They exchange secret glances with each other and speak in a silent language I don't understand. The youngest priestess stares at me a lot. I think her name is Sumire. It suits her because she is dainty with violet eyes.

It's time to wash the floors of the temple. This is my least favorite job. It's the dirtiest and it takes the longest. Bucket after bucket of black water. I wring out the towels so many times my wrist throbs and my knuckles turn raw. My back hurts from arching over and running side to side through the large wooden structure.

It's been uneventful this morning. Nobody passes by me at the sacred grounds. There have been no visitors to the temple either. I sit down to take a break and rest my sore back and red hands. It's hot and I sigh from the heat. I long to sit in the shade of the trees and watch clouds go by or pick flowers in the meadow. The sooner this is done the sooner I can go. With all the momentum I can muster I continue my task. I knock over one of the buckets in my frenzy but I use it to my advantage and run back and forth with a towel under each foot. This isn't how I'm supposed to do it but no one is around to see me. The floor shines now that the dirt and grime is gone.

I rest my hand on my hip and stretch my other arm to the ceiling and rub the small of my back. Now I just have to dump these buckets and wash the towels before hanging them on the line. As I reach for the bucket I notice something. The black water inside is moving. Small ripples spread out into bigger rings. If the water was clear I may not have noticed but in the inky darkness I can make out a quiver.

"Aiya?"

"What is it, Brother Minoru?" I'm still looking at the water.

"Something is coming." His lips are pulled into a tight line.

"I can see it. It's moving the water. Look." I point to the bucket.

"Lady Kiyori was tending to business in the neighboring village. Its people claimed that something was hypnotizing the villagers and leading them into the forest where they would disappear."

"What does that have to do with this?" I keep my eyes on the water and can see it's moving faster.

"I'm sorry to say that it is the same beast plaguing the other village. Lady Kiyori and I sensed a dark presence recently that has only grown stronger." He closes his eyes as he speaks.

"How can we stop it?"

"I don't know if we can. But we will fight with all we have. We have the herbs and the blessed weapons. The priestesses have prepared hundreds of paper charms. Here, take a few." Brother Minoru hands me several pieces of paper with the holy writing.

The water in the bucket sloshes and falls over. We look at each other and then the ground. Trees start sinking into the dirt and rocks tumble after them. Brother Minoru grabs me by the arm and we run.

"To the sacred grounds," he says without emotion. Cedars topple over and oak trees collapse into large cracks forming in the earth. Brother Minoru has us stand back to back between two shrines.

"Aiya, take this." It's a sword in a red leather sheath. One of the blessed weapons. I have never wielded a sword but I don't hesitate to take it.

"Where is Lady Kiyori?" I ask.

"Lady Kiyori and the priestesses went to gather everyone into the middle of the village. When I say so we will make a run for it, okay?"

"Okay," I whisper. The sunny sky is turning dark and a heavy fog rolls in. I can't see more than a foot in front of me.

"Now!"

Brother Minoru holds me by the elbow and we run towards the middle of the village. I worry we may see a monster in the mist but we see no man or beast. A swirling cloak conceals our enemy but also our friends. We weave between houses and shops and duck down behind bushes. We hide against the remaining trees.

"We're almost there," says Brother Minoru.

He doesn't let go of me. Then we hear it. The loud emanating laughter. It sounds full of teeth and hate. Neither of us can tell which direction it's coming from. It is everywhere just like the fog. The sun is being blocked out and a large shadow appears. I look up to see what is casting it. To my horror it's a giant centipede. The dirt gives in around him as he reveals himself. The entirety of his body is wrapped around the village. Hundreds of pointed legs squirm and adjust. His laughter turns into a ferocious roar. The guttural cackle is soon replaced by a wail of anguish. An arrow flies from the fog and into his underbelly.

"Silly mortals, you think your weapons can stop me?" it murmurs.

Its body rejects the arrow which falls out and lands in the grass. Another arrow cuts through the mist and hits him in the head. This one appears to have done more damage than the first for the creature screeches in pain. Brother Minoru charges at it with his sutras and the centipede thrashes, tearing up the land, and nearby structures.

"How dare you! Pathetic little humans," it hisses. Lady Kiyori emerges from the thick clouds and strikes the demon in the face with her sword.

"Perish!" she calls as she leaps again for another hit.

"Just you wait...just you wait," it taunts before retreating into the ground.

"Lady Kiyori!" cries Brother Minoru.

"I'm alright. The priestesses are okay, too."

"Is it really gone?" I ask but no one is listening.

"What about the villagers?" asks Brother Minoru.

"We have them gathered by the shops. The priestesses are in a protective circle around them. I think everyone is fine," Lady Kiyori's voice is feminine but authoritative. I sense something is wrong. Why would a demon that large and powerful retreat so easily? It didn't make sense. I walk into the fog to see if I can find Chiyo. There are hushed voices everywhere and a baby starts to cry. I see the outline of a woman in the mist. She has a bow on her back. It must be Sumire. I call her name but no reply.

"Sumire, is that you?" Still nothing.

"Hello, is anyone there?" I call into the clouds. I'm about to turn around and head back to Lady Kiyori and Brother Minoru but Sumire blocks my path.

"Sumire! You startled me. Are you okay? Is everyone alright?" She stares at me blankly.

"Are you hurt?" Reaching behind her back she grabs an arrow and draws her bow at me. I put my hands up.

"Please don't, Sumire. Why are you doing this?"

We made frequent eye contact in passing. I remember her eyes. Lively and violet just like her name. Right now her eyes are dull and she looks like she is in a daze.

"Aiya...run..." her voice is trembling. The bow is taut as she speaks.

"Sumire–" she fires the arrow but I manage to dodge it.

"Aiya...get...away from me," she says through clenched teeth.

I recall what Brother Minoru said about the beast luring people into the forest. Perhaps the centipede is also responsible for Sumire's behavior. Certain creatures were known to possess the ability to control human minds. I go back in the direction towards Lady Kiyori and Brother Minoru.

"The centipede, I think it's controlling Sumire!" I call.

"Lady Kiyori? Brother Minoru? Where are you?" No reply. I make my way through the demonic aura. It wraps around my arms and legs, sending chills up my spine. Keeping my palm on the handle of the sword I tread with caution. I'm about to call her name but I realize she has her foot on Brother Minoru's chest and her sword to his neck.

"No!" I scream and I tackle her to the ground. She tries to strangle me but I punch her in the face. Lady Kiyori's mouth goes slack and she falls over unconscious.

"Brother Minoru! Are you alright?"

"Yes. Thank you, Aiya," he says, touching his throat.

"The centipede is controlling people. Sumire just tried to kill me."

"I feared this would happen," he says. His voice is hoarse.

"What do we do to defeat it?"

"I'm afraid we can't. The centipede has already burrowed itself below and around the village. It's impossible to move it. This demon will feed on us one by one until there's nothing left." His forehead creases and his eyes are wet with tears.

"What about the others?" I ask.

"If he is a cruel one he is probably toying with them. Entertaining himself before consumption."

"There has to be something we can do! Please don't give up! I don't want to give up, Brother Minoru."

"Do you remember when you first came to our village? You said a demon with white hair and amber eyes brought you here..." He is far away as he speaks. The small smile he wears is out of place.

"Yes, I remember." I could never forget.

"Lady Kiyori said it was the result of something traumatic happening to you. That he was just a dream," he says and his smile grows.

"She told me I should forget about him. That he wasn't real," I say.

"He is real, Aiya. I saw him leave you by the sacred spring. He made no sound as he walked. I managed to catch a glimpse of him. I had never seen gold eyes before." As he says this my heart skips a beat.

Brother Minoru saw the demon that brought me here? I couldn't comprehend it. I wasn't crazy after all? The face that haunts me every night belongs to someone.

"Why did you keep this from me?" I want to be angry with him but I'm not.

"I thought you would be better off if you didn't think about your past. I wished for you to have a happy childhood. It was selfish of me. I'm sorry," he says and begins to cough making his eyes bulge.

"I forgive you Brother Minoru. But tell me, why are you talking about this now?"

"You must find him, Aiya. He has the power to stop the centipede."

"What if he won't help us?"

"I believe he will. He had compassion for you as a child. He rescued you from the demon that terrorized your village. I saw the way he carried you into the sacred grounds. The look on his face. How he set you down so gently. He cared, Aiya."

"How will I find him?"

"Take the blessed weapon into the forest and follow your heart," he says and puts his hand to his chest.

"Follow my heart?"

"Have faith, Aiya. Faith is what keeps us alive." His eyes are closed and he turns away from me. I wish to ask more questions but Brother Minoru is out of answers.

CHAPTER THIRTEEN

The Importance of a Name

My first three days in the forest were rough. I keep the small knife Hajime made for me in my obi. My palm never leaves the handle of the sword and my eyes remain wide open, unblinking. I didn't sleep for two days. In that time I learned the sounds of the trees, the way the wind blew through them. Owls and bats came out at night. Their noises were distinct in the dark. Wandering as an aimless ghost through a sea of green I attempt to follow my heart.

I can forage edible mushrooms but I don't know if I am capable of finding someone who only appears to me in my dreams. I try to remember what Brother Minoru said. During the times I feel weak and cannot bear another step I conjure up his voice. Have faith, Aiya. Faith is what keeps us alive.

Something poisonous bites my ankle but lucky for me Lady Kiyori taught me about medicinal herbs and I find the antidotal plant nearby. The swelling is minimal but it has a fierce sting to it. I camp near a stream where I can use the clean water to drink and cool the burning bite.

I try to rest but think of Chiyo and the others. The centipede was turning brother against brother, sister against sister. I pray for their safety. The stories of the giant centipede repeat themselves in my mind. It could grow massive enough to wrap around mountains. The body was strong but its demonic power was stronger. It is rumored that they feast on human souls. I try not to think of my village cradled in its hundred arms veiled in a blanket of mist. There is a screeching noise coming from the east and I take shelter in the hollow of a tree.

It sounds like the caw of a crow but much louder. From my hiding place I can see the light blue sky. I wait for the owner of the noise to reveal itself. It goes by so quickly all I see is a blur of black feathers. Avoiding popping my head out I lean a bit closer for a better view. Another blur of darkness and then another. Then I see them. Enormous black birds with blood red eyes. Demons. The leader squawks and the others join in.

The horrible sound hurts my head and I duck back in and cover my ears. It reverberates in my chest and my vision becomes blurry. I can't recall how long it went on for but when I wake it's evening. I'm disappointed with myself for not covering more ground during the day. I don't dare roam the woods with no moon tonight. My ankle appears to be healing. The redness has faded and it is no longer tender to the touch. I tell myself the extra rest will be beneficial to my journey and close my eyes.

***

To make up for lost time I take no break from my traveling today. Not even when the afternoon sun sits in the middle of the sky and burns my skin. Thinking about Chiyo and the others, how they took me in, and the birthday party forces me to keep my pace. Over the grassy knolls lined with wisteria trees there is a meadow full of flowers. A scarlet ocean. It's the red spider lilies my mother loved. There is little time to stop and appreciate the flowers but I can't resist. I weave through and run my hand over the tops of them singing to myself.

> *Was it you, was it you*
> *Who left me by the spring*
> *There was a man*
> *I know he saved me but*
> *I see him only in my dreams*
> *Was it you, was it you*
> *Who left me by the spring*

* * *

Allowing myself to pick a small bouquet, I put one behind my ear. I look at them and think of my family. Mother, what would you do? Emi would laugh and say no matter the task it would be easy as long as we had each other. Takara would be six now if he were alive. I wonder if he would prefer persimmons or peaches. Would he have been quiet and serious like me and Father? Or would he have been playful and lively like Emi and Mother? When he was born I was the first to hold him. They let me choose his name.

> *Was it you, was it you*
> *Who left me by the spring*
> *I know your face*
> *But not your name*
> *I've been wondering*
> *Who was he, who was he*

Leaves rustle near the treeline. I assume it's just the wind but I draw my sword anyway. I hear something moving in the bushes and a low animalistic noise. The tip of an orange tail indicates a tiger is in my presence.

"Come out," I demand.

"Feisty," a voice purrs.

"Show yourself."

"No need to be boorish," says a man materializing from the foliage. I see he is the owner of the orange tail. He was no human.

"What do you want?" I ask and he begins circling around me. I keep my eyes on him. My parents taught me to never turn your back to a cat for that is when it will pounce.

"I want to know what a young woman is doing by herself this far out in the forest," he says.

"Why is that of interest to you?"

"Why won't you tell me?" He doesn't stop circling me.

"I'm looking for someone," is all I offer.

"They must be pretty important for you to come all this way," the tiger demon says as he draws out his sentence.

His eyes are penetrating sapphires and the markings on his face and wrist match the stripes on his tail. He wears only blue trousers.

His hair is the brightest orange red I have ever seen. Remarkable to witness but still a predator. He moves his tongue across his fangs.

"Will you let me pass? I won't be a bother," I say as I follow his gaze which is now all over my body.

"Tell me, are you looking for a man?" he growls at me.

"I'm in search of help. My village is under attack," I say. Perhaps my honesty would persuade him to let me go.

"Maybe I can offer my services. But I don't work for free," he says as he examines his claws.

"What do you expect in return?"

"Be mine. Let me have you. As soon as I'm finished I'll drive out whatever is attacking your village. What do you say?"

"I'll pass." I grimace at his suggestion. He finds my answer amusing and lets out a hearty chuckle. I tighten my grip on the sword and plant my feet to ready myself.

"Calm down. I respect your decision to decline. If your man continues to elude you I suspect you'll come find me," he purrs before returning into the cover of the tall grass.

***

Night takes hold of the sky turning it black and blue. The trees are not as dense here and I can see the stars through the branches. They look like hands reaching up to hold the moon. I take cover in between three oak trees. There are boulders and ferns that grow taller than me. A small grassy ring just big enough for one person is my hiding place.

I lean against the textured bark of the trunk. It is sturdy and strong. How I long to be strong and unwavering like a giant oak. Bats squeak above me and their flapping makes me wince. Peeking out from the rocks I see the nocturnal animals. They have glowing gold, green, and red eyes.

There are shadows in the shapes of wildcats and deer. An owl calls from a cedar. She has jade eyes and snowy wings. A sulfurous scent tinges the air and I hear the night life quiet. I strain my ears to listen. A hiss and then a rustling noise frightens me. It's approaching from the left. I lean back but keep my eyes on the path ahead.

The smell gets worse. It's a sickly festering scent. Like something rotting is on fire. I see the origin of the revolting stench. A snake demon with red eyes is slithering by. He is purple with black spikes along his back. The bulbous head rises and the serpent's tongue tastes the air. Its eyes scan the area for movement. I hold my breath.

It doesn't notice me and I don't move until I am sure the creature is gone. An owl calls out to notify us it is safe. Crickets chirp and the flying insects buzz again. Looking up I watch the moon cross the sky. Constellations twist and turn. I fall asleep listening to the flapping, buzzing, and chirping of midnight.

I dream about tiger demons with jewels for eyes. They wear no shirts or shoes and laugh with hearty chuckles. My rest is fitful and incomplete. I try to close my eyes again. Dreaming about centipedes, spiders, and snakes wakes me with a violent shiver. I stand up and stretch to calm myself. Attempting to quell my fear I put my hand over my heart and take a deep breath.

Leaning against the tree I drift away. Not a satisfying slumber. More dreams about cats, snakes, and creatures with wings. Monks and priestesses push me towards the monsters. I fight them and win. The sensation of the knife in my hand startles me awake. I didn't see the amber eyes tonight. This disheartens me.

That sickening smell of death and sulfur again. It stings as I breathe it in. I pinch my nose but feel it coat the inside of my cheeks with its acidic decay. I lay low but look through the leafy ferns. The moon is a delicate sliver and doesn't offer much light. Keeping my sight on the ground I watch for the source of the smell. A rodent is scurrying across the path but is squished by a heavy black boot.

It makes a tiny but resounding scream as the heel hits the dirt and the mouse's blood splatters. The cracking of a thin skull hurts my teeth. The man in the boots pays no mind and keeps walking. I don't see his face. The only glimpse I got of him is the black boots splattering blood and red trousers.

My imagination must be playing tricks on me because I swear I recognize those boots and somehow that scent is familiar. I blame it on the heat and my lack of rest. The sun won't be up for hours. I lean against the boulder and try to sleep. The dreams make little sense. They are an endless path with shadows lurking in all four corners. The red eyed demons smile salacious grins at me. A mouse ends up in the mouth of a snake demon. It's swallowed whole and the rodent slides through the body of the reptile.

I dream about black boots and little fires burning the grass. There are sapphire eyes watching me. Fireflies gather in the shape of Gemini. I hear the wind call my name. There's red silk everywhere. It's smoky and hot. Crimson incense burns throughout the forest and conceals the spirits and demons hiding from me. A centipede falls out of a tree and lands on my shoulder.

This jars me awake. I wipe off the invisible creature and shriek. Covering my mouth I look around and see that it is still dark. This night has been tiring. I wish to travel but I'm afraid of stepping out onto the path at night. The moon has moved, indicating dawn will be here eventually. I pray for Chiyo and the others. This allows me to press into the oak and fade out until the sun rids the forest of darkness.

CHAPTER FOURTEEN

Only Human

Where am I going? I'm beginning to feel foolish. Brother Minoru believed so whole-heartedly but doubt was creeping in. For the past day I've heard twigs breaking and stirring beyond the ferns. I think the tiger demon is following me, waiting for me to cave in. I was repulsed by his proposition but I am more appalled after I started to contemplate it. What if I can't find the man who rescued me? I don't know what I will do then. Agitated with myself and the heat I throw a rock into the bushes.

"Stop following me!" I yell. To my surprise it's a young woman who stands up. She's rubbing her head. I must have hit my mark.

"Hey! What was that for?" she whines at me.

"I am so sorry! I thought you were that tiger demon."

"Oh, Torao? He's a real creep. Watch out for that guy," her voice softens.

As she gets closer I realize she's a demon, too. She appears to be human with the exception of pointy black and red ears on top of her head. A fox demon.

"You know him?" I ask with audible interest.

"Not personally. He thinks he owns this part of the forest. A real big shot," she says and wrinkles up her nose.

"He's certainly full of himself," I say and we both laugh. It's been so long since I smiled.

"My name is Hanako," she says. Now that she was in front of me I could see how beautiful she was.

Hair the color of sparkling starlight and chestnut eyes. She smiles at me which exposes her sharp canine teeth. She notices me staring at them and quickly covers her mouth.

"I apologize. My name is Aiya."

"What are you doing here? Humans don't normally come out this far."

"I'm looking for someone. Can I ask why you were following me?"

"I saw you traveling by yourself. I worried for your safety. There are a lot of dangerous things in the forest," she says in a whisper.

"You worried about me?"

"Well, yeah. I'm also very curious. I couldn't help but see where you were going. I'm sorry." She holds her arm and hangs her head.

"It's okay. I would be curious, too. I'm really sorry I hit you in the head with that rock."

"Who are you looking for? Maybe I can help!" Her face lights up and she looks at me expecting an answer.

"I'm...not sure exactly," I mumble.

"What do they look like?" she asks.

"He has snow white hair and gold eyes. It's been many years since I've seen him," I reply.

"I think I know who you are searching for!"

"You do?" My eyes widen in disbelief.

"His name is Riku. The disgraced wolf prince. A white omega. Rumor has it he used to live with the demon wolf clan in the northern mountains, but now wanders the woods alone." Hanako's voice is ringing in my ears. My heart starts to race. It beats with such intensity it forces the air out of my lungs. I lose my breath.

"A lone wolf?" I ask. My voice sounds like I'm drowning but she doesn't acknowledge it.

"Yes. If a wolf refuses to fight the alpha the rest of the pack will turn on him," she replies. Her tone is sad.

"That's so awful," is all I can say. Was this the person I am looking for?

"I'll help you look for him! I'm not strong like other demons but I can protect you, Aiya."

"Thank you but I can't ask you to assist me. This is my duty.

You've already been too kind," I say and begin to walk away but she stops me.

"Wait, please! Let me help," she grabs my sleeve.

"Why do you insist?"

"Because...I want to be your friend." Hanako smiles at me with warmth. She reminds me of Chiyo. They have the same bubbly voice and affectionate demeanor. I let my heart open to her.

"Let's not waste any time then," I say with genuine delight as me and my new friend search for the white wolf.

***

Hanako is good company. She keeps my mind off the heat with her constant chatter. It doesn't bother me though. I found it comforting to hear her speak.

"Have you always been curious about humans?" I ask.

"Sort of. Our burrow was near a human family with four children. My siblings and I would often play with them. We would show them our fox magic and they'd chase us," she tells me.

"I always thought humans and demons lived in separate worlds. That's a sweet story."

"Their parents didn't like us. We had to play when they weren't around," she admits.

"Oh," I trail off. Hanako is a kindhearted soul. It's hard to imagine someone not liking her.

"That was a long, long time ago," she says and waves it off.

"What is the fox magic you speak of?" I'm becoming more and more interested in demons.

"I can shapeshift but only for short amounts of time. I can also mimic voices. Most of my power is based in illusions. I'm not strong like Torao or the white wolf," she informs me. As she does she transforms and her face becomes my face. She sticks her tongue out at me.

"Hey! No fair!" I laugh. We're too busy laughing to realize someone is standing in our path.

"Pardon us," I say.

He's wearing the fur of a bear. The head is being used as a hood and it drapes over his face. Only his mouth and chin are visible.

"You should turn back," he says.

"Your advice is not necessary," I say as me and Hanako make our way to pass him. She doesn't take her eyes off him.

"It's not safe out here, Katan."

"You have me confused with someone else. My name is Aiya," I retort.

"My mistake," he says. I look back and he isn't there anymore.

"That man is a demon. A powerful one," says Hanako. She continues walking backwards. She won't move her eyes from where he was standing.

"He assumed I was someone named Katan. He probably won't bother us anymore." I keep walking not wanting to stop. Time is not a luxury I possess.

"Yeah, you're probably right."

We keep going until the stars come out. I set up camp and start a fire while Hanako goes out to get food. I ate well since meeting her. She is skilled at finding roots, berries, and catching rabbits. She comes back with a hare in each hand.

"Look! We don't have to share tonight," she beams as she sits down next to me in front of the fire.

"Thank you! These will be delicious," I say.

A majority of my diet had been roots and mushrooms. My body is craving the greasy meat from the rabbit. In the low light of the fire I can see the claws on Hanako's delicate hands. Her canines shred through the meat with little effort. I try not to stare but she is fascinating.

"What are you going to do when we find Riku?" she asks.

"I'm going to ask him for help. My village has been taken over. A giant centipede has embedded himself there. We burn the herbs meant to repel demons daily and we possess blessed weapons but it's too strong. I need him," I whisper the last part.

"How do you know him?" She's looking at me but my eyes don't meet hers.

"On my thirteenth birthday a demon burned my village to the ground. People were in pieces around me. I was frozen, staring into the eyes of my father as he took his last breath. The demon was closing in on me. I felt someone pick me up and start running. I saw his face for only a moment. Then I woke up in a place I had never seen before," I say.

"I'm sorry, Aiya. I didn't know about your family. That's terrible," she says with tears in her eyes.

"It's okay Hanako. Don't cry for me," I say and put my hand on her shoulder. She reaches for me and holds it there.

"I can't help it. We only get one family. Once they're gone they're gone," her voice is shrill this time.

"We might only get one family but I have a best friend in the village, Chiyo. You remind me of her. She is my family now, I would do anything for her. Family can be the people closest to us. The ones that know us inside and out."

"Can we be family?" asks Hanako. Her question catches me off guard. I don't know her well but I can't bear to hurt her feelings.

"We are," I yawn. I lay down and so does Hanako. She takes my hand in hers and I fall asleep.

My brother's birth is on the night of the full moon. The snow is fresh without footprints. It's the winter solstice, a special date. Father hopes for a son. I want a baby brother. Emi and mother wish for another girl.

Mother's hair sticks to the sweat on her face. My father is by her side to the left, Emi and I to the right. She holds on to both me and Father as she pants and groans. Emi offers her cool water and encouragement. We are all together the moment my brother arrives but I see him first, touch him first, and hold him first. Father cries with happiness and claps excitedly.

"It's a boy! It's a boy!" he chants. Emi and mother hug each other while laughing through their tears. I say nothing. He left me speechless. After he calms down and stops crying he looks up at me. I stare into his deep, hypnotizing eyes. They are innocent and pure.

"What do you want to name him, Aiya?" Mother asks me. All four of them look to me and wait patiently for my answer.

"Takara. His name is Takara."

"That's a perfect name," says my father.

"Aiya! Aiya, wake up!" Hanako is hovering over me.

"Sorry, did I oversleep?" I ask, groggy from my dream. My cheeks are streaked with tears.

"No, it's still early. But you kept saying someone's name. Takara, that's your little brother, right?" Her voice is sympathetic.

"Yes. I was dreaming about him. It's been years but I can still remember exactly how I felt the night he was born," I reply as I wipe my face with the sleeve of my kimono.

"You loved him very much. He's important to you." She's thoughtful as she speaks.

"I picked his name. He looked up at me and I knew."

"I still dream about my brothers and sisters, too." This surprises me. I assumed they would still be alive. Demons can live for centuries.

"I never asked you about your family," I admit with obvious guilt.

"It's okay. I didn't want to make you sad. But after what you've told me I realize we have a lot in common."

"Hanako, where are you siblings? What about your parents?"

"My father is still alive. He lives near the coast to the west. He is the elder and leader of the western fox tribe," she confesses. Hanako is a demon fox princess. She studies my astonishment before continuing.

"Fifty years ago we were attacked by a troop of monkey demons. They took over our land. Made their homes in the treetops and destroyed our burrows. Vicious and ruthless beasts that ripped the limbs off my brothers and sisters. One tore my mother's head from her body. My father has powerful magic and he used his foxfire to defeat them. He managed to save me but everyone else was gone."

She rests her head on her knees signaling she is done talking. My new friend had been through so much. I would have never guessed. She always seemed happy and carefree.

"I'm sorry, Hanako. Please forgive my callousness. I had no idea," I try to get out the words but I can't.

I realize this must be how everyone in the village felt. Trying their best to offer comfort or support but unable to find the right thing to say. Maybe Natsume, Hiromi, and Daina really were my friends. They didn't say what I wanted them to say but they went out of their way for me. I vow to never take them for granted again.

"It's okay."

"I'm really glad I met you, Hanako."

"I'm glad I met you, too." She smiles at me and stands. I stretch and dust myself off. The sun rises from the east and the shadows retreat back into the woods.

"When was the last time you saw Riku?" I ask. I have never said his name before. It's shiny and metallic in my mouth. Touching my neck I feel it steal my breath again.

"About a month ago. We are close to the place where I saw him."

"Have you ever spoken to him?"

"No. I've only seen him three times. His eyes are kind but he seems…" her voice trails off.

"Seems what?"

"Like a serious person. His face carries a lot of sorrow," she finishes.

"You think him to be kind though? How can you tell?" I begin nibbling on some radishes as we walk.

"I can just tell. You said so yourself. He saved you from that monster. I think for him to do that he must have a good heart." She walks through a spiderweb and brushes it off without emotion.

"I hope you're right. He's probably forgotten me," I shrug. Hanako is an optimist but I could never be a true believer.

"A wolf never forgets," she says with great confidence.

***

"Hanako, can I ask you something?"

"Sure! Ask me anything."

Her voice is shimmery like her hair. There is a light breeze shaking leaves off the branches. She dances with them and they hang suspended in the air. Time is frozen. They do not fall.

"What is it like?" My question causes her to pause and the leaves drop one by one. She looks puzzled.

"What do you mean?"

"What's it like being a demon?"

I feel like I am being invasive but I can't contain my curiosity. Hanako stares at me for a moment. Her ears twitch and she wrinkles up her nose. She gives me an explosive laugh. I can't help but laugh when she laughs.

"I'm not sure how to answer that, Aiya. What's it like being human?" Hanako has thick but short eyelashes. They remind me of bird feathers. Her face is round. It makes her appear innocent and childlike.

"You're right. I apologize," I start but Hanako cuts me off.

"No, no! It's okay. I am curious about your world as well," she says and wiggles her nose. This eases me. She's not upset.

"I haven't been around demons much. I am learning new things every day," I say. We keep walking. The summer sun beams down through the thick canopy causing white spots throughout the dark woods.

"I know you were afraid of me at first but I'm glad you gave me a chance," says Hanako in the sweet way she says most things. I chide myself on my rudeness. The way she covered her canines as I stared at them. She is very beautiful despite being a demon.

"Thank you for helping me. I don't know how I could ever repay your kindness."

"You don't have to repay me. I'm your friend, silly!"

She picks up two handfuls of black inky hair and dances next to me. We skip through spotted sunshine and shadows until we reach an open field. The tall grass is shades of jade and emerald. In the distance the mountains to the north are three indigo peaks. Hanako takes off rolling down the hill, spinning, and giggling to herself. She is a girl who can make every moment magical. There is no dull hour with her at my side.

"Hanako! Wait for me," I laugh and I join in on the fun.

The last time I did anything like this I was with Emi. We were playing on the hill near our house. It was lined with magnolias and oak trees. I remember Emi always wanting to race down the small grassy knoll. It seemed so big to us back then. She would jump up and shriek when she won. I let her win all the time just to see her dance and jump with joy.

I meet Hanako at the bottom of the hill and we laugh as we lay in the grass cheek to cheek. Fluffy clouds pass by. We get lost in them. They spread out into ocean waves and wild horses. One looks like a teapot. A creamy bunny passes over us and is moved by the breeze.

Hanako points to a dragonfly and it lands on her hand. She glistens blue green and has pretty black legs that grip the tip of Hanako's finger. We admire her clear rainbow wings. Another dragonfly nears us. He is luminous red and yellow. They are fire and ice. She walks onto Hanako's wrist to say goodbye before she goes off with him. I get up and stretch my arms to the sky.

"That was amazing!" says Hanako with glee.

She grabs my hand and we run through the emerald field just to feel the wind on our faces. Even though it's blazing hot I feel refreshed. Out of the corner of my eye I see Hanako skipping with her eyes closed. Her starlight hair catches the sun and a brilliant light shines around her like a halo.

Dusk is upon us. We find a safe place to settle down. Staring into the fire we sit with our thoughts until the stars come out. Crickets chirp and bats squeak beyond the treeline. It's breezy but nice. The night air is a floral kiss. It's dewy and sweet. A white flower opens and wispy seeds glow gold as they are carried by the wind. They are magical. It looks like they are being guided to the waxing crescent and are pulled into the spectral plain. I long to see what's right in front of me.

"Wow," I whisper. Hanako can tell this interests me.

"The forest is dangerous but it's beautiful," she says in earnest. The moon rises over the cedars and camphor trees. It's only a sliver but it entrances me. I can't stop staring at it. Does the man who rescued me stare up at the moon when I do?

"I was too afraid to take one step into the forest. After my village was attacked I ran into it without a second thought," I admit as I take a bite out of a peach.

Hanako is nibbling on a plum. An apprehensive air takes hold of me as I remember Hajime, Sumire, and the others.

"You are a brave girl," she says. I laugh at her remark.

"I don't feel very brave."

I've been terrified out of my mind most of the time but I keep it to myself. No sense in complaining or giving in to the fear. I have to save my village. There is no time to be afraid.

"You are though."

"You think so?"

"I know so. I've never seen a human all the way out here. Especially one as pretty as you." She is genuine with her words.

"Thank you."

I lay down and count the stars. Touching my face I think of the constellation splashed across my nose and cheeks.

CHAPER FIFTEEN

On My Way to You

The forest is expansive and endless. There is no limit to its beauty or its depth. We wander in search of the white wolf who saved me. I dream about him again. The disheveled white hair covers his handsome face but the gold eyes pierce through. For some reason the shadow in my dream frightens me more than it used to. It feels ominous and malicious.

There are muddy puddles with pretty flowers that remind me of milk and blood. They are strange and appear out of place but I like them. I think I enjoy seeing something beautiful grow from the mud that is dark and uninviting. There is something to be said about beauty in unexpected places.

Hanako and I haven't had any luck finding Riku. I feel this connection to him but I can't summon him. It's like he is just out of my reach. Does he sense that I am in the forest? Did he know I was looking at the moon last night? I pick buttercups and daisies to make a floral necklace. It's not as hot as yesterday and I enjoy the respite from the heat. My cheeks are pink from the summer sun. I feel my long eyelashes tickle my face where the freckles are.

"Aiya! Come look." Hanako is pointing to a pond that is more green than blue. It is lined with daisies and daffodils. We kneel down and upon further inspection I see orange and white bodies. There are two medium sized koi fish swimming in circles around each other. One has a black tail and red face. The other is mostly white with thin fins that sparkle. This one has a horn on its head.

"What is he?" I ask and point to the horned koi.

"From the looks of it he appears to be a koi knight."

"A koi knight?"

"There are regular koi like this one here with the black tail but then there are koi kings, queens, and knights. They have horns." Hanako puts her hand in the water and strokes the koi knight. He doesn't seem to mind.

"How are they different from the regular koi?"

"The knights protect the koi with no magic from other predators. The queens give birth to the knights. Kings are the only ones who can mate with a queen. They are harmless for the most part. As long as you don't disturb the koi they won't hurt you."

I must look surprised because Hanako holds my shoulder and points to the knight. She takes my hand and has me pet the chubby creature, "See, he isn't bad. Just different."

"I never thought I'd see anything like this," I say under my breath.

"There is always more to see if we are willing to open our eyes."

I meet Hanako's chestnut gaze and sense she is telling me a secret but I don't understand it. We walk arm in arm and I sing to the birds. They repeat my song. This pleases Hanako.

"Did you like that?" I ask with a laugh. Hanako is jumping with excitement.

"Yes! That was wonderful. I didn't know you could do that," she giggles.

"I like to sing," I confess.

"You do? About what?" Her face is expectant and innocent but I feel my cheeks burning up and not from the warm weather.

"I sing about him," I admit in a small voice.

"Can I hear it? Please?" She is too sweet to say no to.

Was it you, was it you
Who left me by the spring
I know your face
But not your name
I've been wondering
Who was he, who was he

* * *

Hanako stares at me with disbelief. She stops us on the path. The sun is high in the sky and the shadows sit still as I wait for her to speak.

"Wow, you have the most beautiful voice." Her hands are clasped. She is sincere.

"Thank you." I am sheepish about sharing my song but I know Hanako will guard it with her heart. It's a childish wish but I hope Riku hears me.

***

To combat the afternoon sun we get up before dawn to travel. Our routine has been to go as far as we can first thing in the morning to avoid the sun. We take breaks near water or in the shade of the trees until the heat passes. After that we go as far as we can until dusk. Then I start the fire and Hanako forages for dinner.

Our schedule has been effective and productive. Everything seems to be asleep as we walk this morning. I can hear water and usher Hanako towards the sound. As we emerge from the treeline we come upon a river. To the left is a cliff resulting in a waterfall. The rapid water flows towards large rocks at the bottom.

"Let's take a break to wash up and rest," I suggest.

Hanako doesn't argue and begins splashing water on her face and rubbing profusely. I scrub my hands and face. We sit with our feet in the water and feel the movement lift and carry the dirt away.

"This is nice," Hanako sighs. I agree and we watch clouds go by with dreamy eyes.

"You really shouldn't be out here," says a deep voice.

We turn to look at the intruder. It's the man in the bear fur. His hood is still up even though it's scorching hot. I stand up and Hanako does as well.

"I'm not who you think I am. Why do you keep bothering us?" I hiss.

"You have always been Katan to me," he says as he steps closer.

"I already told you, my name is Aiya. I don't know who Katan is," I spit at him.

"Listen to my voice. You have known me for a long time. Go back.

Remember me, Aiya." Hanako is stiff and her eyes narrow at the man.

"I'm sorry but you are confused," I say. I have my hand on the sword and ready myself to fight.

"I don't seem familiar? Not even a little?" he asks with disappointment.

"Why should you be familiar to me?"

He removes the bear head from his face. Long black hair spills out from the hood. He has red eyes and pointed ears. I study his tan face which is decorated with a smirk.

"Do you remember me now?"

"No–" but as the word leaves my mouth an image comes to mind.

My father and I were near the pond where the hydrangeas grew. I used to count the flowers as a child. Father pointed to me as he was talking to this man. I try to pick out more details but the memory fades.

"I can tell by the look on your face you do know me," he laughs.

"You knew my father," I say. Hanako has been still as a statue, her eyes never moving from the demon.

"More like your father knew me."

"Who are you?"

"I'm Kasai."

"Why do you keep calling me Katan?"

"A very long time ago your father made a deal with me. He was a poor rice farmer and his crops had gone bad. That meant no money and no food for you or your mother or sister. So he asked me for my help," he says in a syrupy voice.

"What does that have to do with me?"

"He gave you to me, Katan. At the time you were eight years old. He promised you to me on your thirteenth birthday. As long as I made sure his crops grew plentiful you would be mine," he says with a snarl.

"No. My father wouldn't do that to me!" I shout.

"He did. I was going to change your name and alter your life. You belong to me," he growls.

"You're lying! My father loved me!"

"He did love you. You were dear to him. Unfortunately, he was a weak man. Giving you up so easily. All he had to do was let me take you. Your father was weak his whole life, especially the day he rescinded his promise!"

Kasai's face is wild. His laughter reminds me of crackling fire. I draw my sword.

"I don't belong to anyone," I say. Hanako grabs my shoulder before I can rush the demon.

"Aiya, do you trust me?" she asks as her chestnut eyes bore into mine.

"Yes," I reply.

"Then get on my back," she says. I do as she tells me and she takes off with supernatural speed. I can hear Kasai following us.

"Hanako?"

"Hold on tight!" she yells and as she does we dive off the cliff down the waterfall.

I clutch onto her neck so hard I fear I may strangle her. She puts out her arms and in each hand is a feather. I close my eyes preparing to hit the rocks below but we never reach them. Opening one eye I see we're still in the air.

"Hanako! You can fly?" I ask dumbfounded.

"Not really. I can glide using bird feathers. I'm glad I picked them up earlier. They sure came in handy," she says.

I look behind us and see Kasai standing at the ledge. The bear's head is covering his face again.

"This is amazing," I say in awe of my new friend's capabilities.

"Here is where it gets kind of tricky. Since I can only glide it's going to be a bit of a rough landing," says Hanako. The treetops below are coming closer into view.

"Slow down!" I shriek.

"I'm trying!" she cries and we both cut through the canopy of trees and fall into the dense thicket.

***

There is very little light coming through the cover of leaves and thick branches. It's hard to focus my vision. All of the green hues and bark blend together and swirl. I have to get up but I can't. My breath is coming in short and shallow. Putting my arms out I slowly raise my torso off the ground. I must have had the wind knocked out of me. Willing myself to rise I take four deep breaths and lift myself a bit, then I take four more. Checking my body I see no broken bones, only bruises, and minor cuts. I still have the small knife in my obi and the sacred sword. After I stand and steady myself I look in all directions for Hanako. I don't know how long I've been unconscious.

"Hanako!" I call.

Birds fly out from a thousand different hiding places. I continue startling the creatures of the forest with my voice.

"Hanako! Where are you?"

Even though it's daytime it's dark in this part of the woods. Only spots here and there of the sun come through.

"Hanako! Are you okay?"

My voice echoes through the foliage. I try to piece together what happened. We lost control in the canopy of the trees, crashing through layers of branches. I hope she's close. She could have been calling my name while I was out and went ahead. I decide to keep going north towards the mountains. Perhaps she would be on that path.

Even though we only met four days ago I have become quite fond of Hanako. I miss her bubbly chatter. She is sweet and never selfish. Chiyo and her would get along. Thinking about Chiyo and the village brings on a new wave of dread and great sadness. I need to get back to them. I have to find Hanako. In my desperation I continue to call Hanako's name and disturb everything in the forest. I catch a glimpse of red and black and my heart swells.

"Hanako? Is that you?" I run in the direction of the bright colored fur.

"Were you looking for somebody?" It's Torao. He is sprawled out in a patch of sun.

"Not you," I snap and turn to leave.

"Oh, but we could have so much fun. Come back here," he purrs.

"No thank you." There is ice in my voice.

"My offer still stands. I could really save you the trouble. Besides, I'm stronger than that little fox anyways."

"Are you stronger than the wolf demon, Riku?" I ask with curiosity. Torao grooms his claws for a moment before he answers.

"I'm a powerful demon, sure. I can't transform like he can though.

Are you more of a dog person than a cat person?" he asks. As he stretches I can see his light skin ripple over the large muscles in his arms and chest.

"What do you mean by transform?"

"His true form is a colossal wolf. Stands taller than the cedars before you," says Torao without looking away from his claws. There's no doubt Riku could defeat the centipede.

"I have to find my friend. Goodbye."

"I'll be waiting for you, little mouse," he says. I shudder at his blatant lascivious comment.

I'm intent on finding Riku. Everything else fades away. Hanako is still out there and I hope to find her but my faith in the white wolf saving the village is renewed. He could transform into a creature bigger than the cedar trees that touch the sky. I remember what Brother Minoru said, that it was apparent the demon cared for me.

Would he be kindhearted like Hanako? He could have left me in the village to burn but he didn't. Does he ever wonder about me?

It was Kasai's shadow I saw approaching, coming to collect me. I understood what my father meant now. His last words, "Aiya, I love you. I'm so sorry." He knew the destruction of our village was his fault.

I hate my father for giving me up. Yet I couldn't hold onto that anger. Kasai was right, my father was a weak man. He was reckless and let his fear drive him to give away his first born daughter as tribute. He rescinded his promise and our village was turned to ash. Everyone we had ever known was murdered. Regardless, I loved him. He was still my father.

Lost in my thoughts I don't notice the buzzing and slithering sounds around me. Little demons everywhere. They resemble insects and rodents but their eyes are red and their mouths are lined with jagged teeth.

"Get back!" I say and draw my sword.

The blessed weapon slows the weaker beasts. They stalk me, wary of the sword. I begin walking backwards as I slash the air and ground.

"Stay away from me," I hiss at them.

I can't fight them all. Despite being tiny demons there are too many. I wish Hanako was here. She would know what to do. Her cleverness saved me from Kasai. How could I ever repay her kindness? I haven't even been able to give her proper thanks. I swing the sword from side to side, keeping the demons at bay. I can't keep this up forever though. The smaller demons get stronger and more persistent as the sun starts going down.

"No! Stop!"

My wrist aches from fighting off the horde. Their beady red eyes stare up at me. The scratching noises their tiny legs make moving across the dirt and rocks gives me a headache. The slithering and flapping is getting louder.

"Hanako!" I cry. With my left hand I take out the knife from my obi.

"Hanako, please! I need you."

Red eyed flies surround me. I am trying to be strong. The village is counting on me. Only I can bring the white wolf.

Dusk is here. The last of the sun sets in the west. Glowing red eyes and vicious mouths are ready to devour me. No, this can't be how it ends. My village, my people, my friend; they are my responsibility. My family is dead, I don't want anybody else to die.

"Riku!" I don't know why I call for him but I do.

I slash the air with the knife and graze the ground with the sword. The chirping of the insects and rodents is sickening. I knew I was risking my life coming out here. There were undeniable consequences. I was lucky to have met Hanako. She kept me safe and helped me search for a ghost. Her smile reminded me of Chiyo's. I am not ready to give up. Brother Minoru believed in me, so I believe in myself. My tenacity has gotten me this far. I take in a deep breath and brace myself.

"Riku!" I yell his name into the wind.

The air is vibrating with the hum of a thousand wings. I watch as the last of the sun disappears over the hill. I step backwards again and my foot kicks a rock. I hear it bounce twice and then nothing. Behind me is the edge of a cliff. In my efforts to fight the demons I didn't pay enough attention to where I am going.

They continue to inch closer but I have nowhere left to go. One of the bigger creatures lunges at me and knocks me off my feet. Have faith, Aiya. Faith is what keeps us alive. My hair billows around me creating a curtain of black ink. I close my eyes and say his name one more time.

CHAPTER SIXTEEN

Every Promise Has a Price

I'm running through the burning village. Where was I earlier? I can't remember. All I know is it's my birthday and everything is being consumed by the flames. I can't find my father. Everyone's eyes are wide open as they rush past me.

"He's evil! We have to run!" a woman screams.

"Quickly now! Stay close," says an older man to his family. No one is looking at me. What are they talking about?

"Father! Where are you?" I call.

Is my mother okay? What about Emi and Takara? Their faces aren't among the scrambling men and women. I can hear children crying. Takara, are you safe? Please, please, be safe. The roaring red and yellow fire sounds like it's laughing as it spreads. The crowd of people thins out and there are only a few stragglers and myself left. A boy my age stops me.

"Go the other way. There is something horrible back there," he says. I look at him and see he has freckles, too.

"I need to find my family," I say.

"Don't," he urges.

He lets me pass after a moment but he stands in place. The smoke conceals him and he vanishes from sight. The black fog is thicker here. This must be where the fire started. I can't see more than a few feet ahead of me. I dart through the darkness. I wonder what the boy meant? What did he see?

In the light of the flames I find a small toy on the ground. I pick it up and inspect it. It could have been any child's but I knew this one was Takara's. After he was born I carved his name into the wood of the red and blue spinning top. It shakes in my hands as I turn it over to reveal my handwriting.

"No," I whisper and drop it in the dust.

I panic and fly through the fog like a bird. My stomach is churning with my racing thoughts. My heart beats hard enough to escape my chest. My breaths are labored, full of smoke and dread. I approach the miserable scene and vomit. Human heads and limbs are strewn about on the ground. The once green grass is soaked in blood. There's dozens of bodies. Pieces of everyone I ever knew lay in a heap.

"I love you, Aiya. I'm so...I'm so sorry." Father's hand is lifeless in mine.

"Please don't leave me." I can't bear the pain. Let the demon kill me. His shadow is approaching. How could I go on without them? I don't want to live anymore. Dying could not hurt more than this.

"We have to go," he says. I could never forget his face.

"Who are you?"

"No one." I wake with a start. The ghost with gold eyes is looking down at me.

"Riku?"

"How do you know my name?" His voice is gravelly.

"I see you every night in my dreams," I say and sit up. I touch my hips and neck. I feel my head for wounds.

"What are you doing out here?"

"Looking for you," I reply. He watches me with bewilderment. I'm sure I must appear quite strange to him.

"Here, drink this." He offers me water. Up close I see he has white eyelashes.

"Thank you," I choke.

We're not near the ledge where I fell. The northern mountains are much closer. This is a different part of the forest I haven't seen before.

"Why are you looking for me?" he asks. He stands away from me and turns towards the mountains.

"I need your help. A giant centipede has taken over my village. We can't fight him. Please, Riku." I clutch the water container and try to act dignified even though I'm nervous.

"Why my help?" He doesn't look at me. I'm glad he doesn't.

"Do you remember me?" There is a long silence between us. Perhaps Hanako was wrong. Maybe wolves do forget. Riku closes the gap between us and stands over me. He reaches the tops of the cedars as a wolf and towers over me as a person. It's hard to look right at him.

"Yes," he finally answers.

"I know I should be thankful and I have no right to ask you but I need to know. Why did you save me all those years ago?"

"I was in the forest near your village when I smelled the fire. It was too late by the time I got there. Almost everything had been destroyed. I was about to leave but I saw Kasai, a fire demon who enjoys playing games with humans. He preys on the weakness in people's hearts. I couldn't let him take you," says Riku. The sun is in his eyes and he lowers his gaze. I wish to touch his face. The urge confuses me.

"You brought me to Lady Kiyori and Brother Minoru's village because you wanted me to be safe. You must have chosen them for a reason. They raised me well and took care of me. Please, help me save them."

"Were you happy there?" His question surprises me. I am touched by his thoughtfulness.

"Yes, I was happy. My family is irreplaceable but they took me in as their sister, daughter, and friend. Look," I take off the bracelet and place it in his hand.

"Cherished," he says to himself.

"Will you help me defeat the centipede?"

I watch him turn the bracelet over in his palm. It sparkles and I feel myself grin. The wolf demon did care. Brother Minoru and Hanako were right. The kindness reflects in his face even though he doesn't smile. It's his soft gold eyes that hold empathy.

"Let's go," he says and starts walking so fast I almost have to run to keep up with him.

***

Riku doesn't talk much but I don't mind. We are both quiet people and travel in comfortable silence. I can't stop looking at him though. Like Hanako he is fair and appears unreal. In contrast to his light complexion and white hair he wears a high collared black bodysuit with long sleeves and armor. His obi is blue green with flecks of gold. I try not to stare but I am intrigued by his eyes that are different from mine. They are wide set like the foreigners I've seen only a handful of times. He has a distinct appearance that's alluring.

The sword that he carries looks more daunting than anything Tetsuma ever created. A demon must have crafted it because no human could ever wield it. I've been waiting to meet him and I have countless questions but I keep them locked up inside. He agreed to help me and I don't want to bother him.

I think about Hanako. The night she asked if we were family keeps popping into my head. Back then I didn't mean it but I realize she had become like a sister to me in such a short amount of time. How I looked forward to her effervescent chatter and felt the warmth in her voice as she spoke to me. Without intimidation or hesitation she'd take my hand like I was her best friend in the world. I pray she's okay. Lost in my own world I'm not paying attention when Riku stops abruptly and I bump into him.

"Oh, sorry. What is it, Riku?" I ask. He doesn't turn around. I step back feeling shy about invading his space.

"I never asked you your name," he says.

"My name is Aiya," I reply. We keep walking through the shadows of the trees until we come upon a field of wildflowers. The breeze moves them with gentle breaths. Hues of pink, yellow, and white blend together creating a radiant glow against the jade grass.

"Let's take a break," he announces as he leans against the trunk of a tree in the shade. I agree and wander a bit further into the meadow. Some of the flowers are especially tall reaching my knees and tickling my legs.

The sun feels good on my face and arms. A welcomed change after nothing but the coolness of the forest. I don't like the heat but today is perfect and doesn't burn my skin. I choose a spot with more white than pink and lie down. Their stems sway with my movements and the petals fall like raindrops. Flower faces hang over me and I breathe in their sweetness. I put my palms down in the grass and feel my body relax. It's unintentional but I drift away.

"I love you, Aiya. I'm so...I'm so sorry," Father's hand falls away from mine. I don't want to live anymore. I wait for death. There is a hand on my shoulder. I turn to see a man wearing the fur of a bear, the head covering his face. Father, how could you do this to me? I don't want to leave with this man but he pulls me away and kneels down so we are face to face. From his mouth slithers the tongue

of a serpent and it begins wrapping around me.

"Don't worry, Katan. You're with me now." His voice is familiar. The fire encircles us and I can't see anything beyond the flames.

"You can run but you can't hide." My breathing is constricted from the smoke and the serpent tongue squeezing my middle. His tan face is young and handsome but his smile is perverse. He disgusts me. I spit at him and it hits below his right eye.

"Mouse," he calls me through a hysterical fit. As he laughs the flames spread. The serpent tongue enters my mouth and chokes me from the inside.

"Aiya," It's Riku's voice. I like the sound of my name on his lips.

"I must have fallen asleep," I mutter and try to shake off the nightmare.

Riku always saves me before Kasai gets there. I worry that maybe he has the power to invade my dreams. Or perhaps it's because I knew what my father had done. I rub my eyes and feel that they are wet. There is a growing sense of embarrassment as Riku stares at me. I fix my hair and drink some water to calm myself.

"Aiya, I've been wanting to tell you something."

"What is it?"

"I'm sorry. I wish I reached your village sooner."

"It's not your fault, Riku."

"I know," he replies.

Through the bangs that cover his face I can see he has a deep crease in his forehead. He felt guilty. I don't want him to feel that way.

"It was my father that brought the fire demon," I confess, "his crops went bad. Kasai offered him a solution but in return he wanted me. On the day Kasai was supposed to collect me, my father changed his mind. This enraged him and he burned the village to the ground," I tell him. Now Riku seems really worried.

"We better get going," he says and helps me to my feet.

***

Riku wants to travel through the night. I think what I told him about Kasai concerns him more than he lets on. I can't see in the dark but he can. He allows me to hold his hand to steady myself. He has slowed his pace so I can keep up. There isn't any moonlight in the forest. Every now and then I spy red and green reflector eyes. They do not announce their presence or try to attack. A white owl flies over us. Her eyes glow yellow and gold in the dark like Riku's. Mice scurry back and forth on the trail and one of them ends up in the mouth of the owl. The poor creature's tail hangs from its beak.

I'm so tired. I haven't been sleeping much. The dreams about Kasai scare me more than the monsters that lurk in the darkness. If he really can see me through my dreams then it is best to avoid sleep entirely. Remembering the feeling of the serpent tongue in my mouth sends a painful shiver through my body. I feel paranoid and look over my shoulder. Is he watching me right now? A twig snaps to our left and I gasp.

"It's okay. It's just a deer," Riku assures me. I tell myself to be strong and we continue walking. I can see stars through an opening in the treeline. We exit and find ourselves standing at a cliff. Across the way is the waterfall where I last saw Hanako. There's a weight in my stomach every time I think about her. I become more and more convinced I won't ever see her again. A wolf howls from the northern mountains. Its voice echoes in the pitch dark.

"Do you ever answer?" I ask.

"No," he replies. I know I shouldn't but my curiosity gets the better of me.

"What happened there?" I ask, still looking to the mountains. I expect Riku not to answer me but he does.

"Wolf demons have kept the tradition of killing the alpha to ascend to the throne. My father got too old and he chose me to lead. I refused and it was my older brother that took over. He resented me for not fulfilling our father's wishes. My brother challenged me and I declined. My siblings began abusing me soon after," he says. Riku's story hurts my heart.

"Why did you refuse?"

"I had no interest in leading. I didn't want to kill my father or fight my brother."

Riku takes silent steps and I follow behind. The wolf howls again in the distance but he doesn't stop. I'm struggling and stumbling over my feet.

"Here, let me carry you," says Riku as he kneels down.

"You don't have to do that. I'm fine," I say.

"You're exhausted and you can't see in the dark. Let me help you." His voice is gruff.

"Okay," I agree and put my arms around his neck.

I worry I may have upset him with my questions. My thighs rest in his hands and I'm wary of his claws. His steps are measured and even. It almost feels like I'm floating. Being this close I notice he smells like pine needles. I can feel the heat radiating from his skin. Resting my head on his shoulder I watch the patches of stars through the canopy. Without meaning to, I slip into a deep sleep.

It's dark even though it's daytime. There are red tones behind my eyelids. My eyes are closed. They open and I see I am in the hollow of a tree. How did I get here? The last thing I remember is being with my father. We were having tea where the hydrangeas grow. I was telling him how excited I was for my birthday. Looking around I notice I'm not anywhere near the village. My head hurts. In a confused daze I walk at a snail's pace home.

I love my new kimono. It's a delicate pink with small floral designs. Mother and Emi gave it to me this morning. They did my hair before we had our breakfast outside. There are a lot of gaps in my memory. First I was there, now I am here. The aftertaste of bitter herbs and spices is strong in my mouth. Father gave me a special birthday tea. What did he put in it? Why am I all the way out here?

I wander through the forest and hope I am heading in the right direction. Above the treetops I see black clouds, then there is the smell of smoke. I run as fast as I can. As I'm running I trip over the roots of a tree. I look up to see my village burning to the ground.

"It can't be," I whisper but no one is around. I have to find my family. How did I become separated from them? I get ready to enter the flames when someone grabs my wrist.

"Where do you think you're going, Katan?"

"I'm not Katan! Get off of me!"

"You've always been Katan to me," he snarls. He has fangs and dark red eyes. His face is attractive but horrifying.

"Stop! I don't know you!" I cry and attempt to break away.

"But I know everything about you."

"Let me go!"

"You'll never escape me," he says as he pulls me into The Underworld.

I open my eyes. The sun is out. I must have been sleeping for quite some time.

"Riku?" I rasp. My nightmare caused me to lose my voice. He sets me down. I'm braver in the dark and I avoid making eye contact.

"Why didn't you wake me?" I ask. It had to be late morning.

"You needed rest," he replies.

"Thank you," I say.

I am sincere but upset with myself for falling asleep. Kasai was messing with my mind. Walking helps make me feel better. I ponder sharing my dreams with Riku but I look at him and I see he's somewhere else. I keep my nightmare to myself. To our right I see orange and black. I wince and prepare myself for what's about to come.

"There you are. My little mouse." Torao growls at me from his perch in the trees.

"Go away," I shoo him and keep walking. Riku stays still, locking eyes with Torao.

"I see you found your man," he teases as he sways his tail back and forth. It's obvious that this is amusing to him.

"What I do is none of your business," I shout and quicken my pace.

"Suit yourself. You smell like a dog now anyway," he says.

Torao turns his nose up at us before disappearing into the sea of green. I fold my arms and keep my head down. What a nasty thing to say! The tiger demon's comment vexes me more than it should. I can hear Riku next to me.

"What was that about?" he asks.

"Nothing. Just a creepy cat is all," I reply. He accepts this answer but doesn't stop looking at me for a long time.

CHAPTER SEVENTEEN

Every Thing You Do For Me

The bamboo is as tall as the trees. It has paths that lead every which way. We maneuver through the maze's twists and turns. An easy place to get lost but I feel safe with Riku. I don't know him. We have barely spoken, yet I trust him. The only sound is his boots hitting the ground. I swear I see something behind us but I convince myself it's just my imagination. Weaving through the bamboo I hear something faint over our footsteps. It sounds like a woman's voice. I stop walking and strain my ears to hear.

"Aiya! Don't fall behind," he calls to me.

"I'll be right there," I reply.

The bamboo is bent at the top forming tunnels the further we go. Riku leads us to a dead end and we turn around to catch a glimpse of long black hair.

"Did you see that?" I ask.

"I did." Riku draws his sword. He motions for me to stay behind him as he peeks around the corner. There is laughter to our right.

"Who is she?"

"I don't know. Stay next to me," he orders and I follow as close as I can without bumping into him.

We take a hard left and run. I hear laughter all around me. There is no distinction which direction it's coming from. I'm looking everywhere for her. This isn't an ordinary woman. A flash of black hair enters the corner of my eye and I turn to look. I'm frozen in my tracks. A woman in a white kimono with long black hair is smiling at me. The grin is unnatural. I know this must be some kind of trick but I can't move. Her hair is shiny and straight. It covers her eyes.

The ground moves beneath me. I am aware of everything that's happening but I can't move my body. Staring at the woman I notice that she is attached to something. The sun hits it in certain spots and reveals a white thread. It's controlling the woman and she is not what she seems. Her head lolls to the side and her limbs go slack. The dirt is caving in around her. From a crater in the earth emerges an enormous black spider. The woman was only its lure. I've heard stories of spider demons. Legend goes that if an orb spider lives to be four hundred years old it's given unique abilities.

The tunnels make more sense now. This is its hunting ground. All the dead ends and unnecessary trails gave it the advantage. The paths were clear and methodical. It must have used its feminine puppet to lure men into the maze and eat them for decades. It casts its web at me and uses it as a net, pulling me closer. The spider creature is hideous with jagged black legs and dozens of red eyes. It roars and I see venom dripping from its fangs. My fingers hurt from pulling at the net but I can't break it. The spider is right in front of me now. I cross my arms over my face.

It lets out another roar spitting venom all over. It rears up on its back legs and the forest floor rumbles. I close my eyes. The beast lets out another scream and I'm sure that this is the end. Then I hear someone run past me. It's Riku! He's fighting the spider. It moves to strike but it's no match for him. He buries the sword in its head and the creature collapses. Riku slices through the web with ease and brings me to my feet.

"Are you okay?" he asks. My voice is gone again so I nod. He helps me up and doesn't let go of my hand until we exit the maze. My heart keeps racing even after we're far away from the spider's den. Halfway through the day the forest begins to look familiar. We are getting close. I see the wisteria trees that marked my third day in the forest.

"I'm going to get some water," I announce and stop at the river. My heart will not slow down. I splash cool water on my face and run it through my hair. I close my eyes and take a few deep breaths.

"Aiya!" Someone is calling my name. I stand up and my eyes search in every direction.

"Aiya! Is it really you?" It's Hanako!

"Hanako!"

My voice is watery. I would never hesitate to call her family again. I vow to be a better friend. She comes running at me from across the river. Her embrace nearly knocks me off my feet. She rests her head on my shoulder and squeezes me.

"Aiya, you're okay! I was so worried I'd never see you again." I can feel her crying.

"We're together now. That's all that matters," I assure her. Hanako lifts her head up and stares at Riku.

"You found him," she whispers in amazement.

"More like he found me," I laugh. He steps closer to join us.

"Riku, this is Hanako. She helped me when I first began my journey. Her cleverness saved me from Kasai," He nods at her and she gives him a polite bow. Her jaw tenses.

"I have to tell you something, Aiya."

"What is it?"

"After you and I were separated I saw Kasai looking for you. He was getting too close so I shapeshifted and mimicked your voice. I lured him as far to the south as I could. I came back to get you but you were gone. I followed your scent to the cliff. I thought you were dead," she clings to me and I stroke her starlight hair to comfort her.

"It's okay, Hanako. I'm right here." I'm overjoyed to be reunited with my friend but hearing Kasai's name makes me nauseous.

"We should continue. Your village is close," Riku says to me. Hanako pulls away but holds my hands for a moment longer.

"Thank you for taking care of Aiya. She is like a sister to me," says Hanako as she flashes him a large grin. Riku takes the lead and me and Hanako follow with her elbow laced with mine.

The sun begins to set and he kneels, indicating it's time for him to carry me. I feel like I've walked a thousand miles. My body is made of wood and metal. The harder I fight my dreams the more vivid they become.

"Hanako, can you see in the dark?" asks Riku.

"You bet," she answers.

"Let's not waste any time then," he says.

Night takes over and right before I fall asleep I see the mossy green glow of Hanako's eyes.

We're in the meadow. Summer is here and the field is a rainbow. I'm showing Takara all the different flowers. Holding him close I point and name them: camellia, magnolia, hydrangea. He laughs and kicks his tiny legs. With eager hands he reaches for their colorful petals. I pick a few buttercups and hand them to him.

"What do you think, Takara? Pretty like the sun," I say and twirl the flowers under his chin casting a yellow glow. I do it to myself and when I show him this trick his eyes light up. I show him all the magic I know. How to cast yellow shadows with buttercups and where to find salamanders. I sing to the birds and wait for them to answer. We watch the lotus that sinks to the bottom with the setting sun and find flowers that only bloom at night. As I walk with him *close to my chest the fireflies come out to play. I stop to admire them. Their light reflects in Takara's eyes. He is enchanted by them. We both are. I touch the tip of his pink nose.*

"You are precious. That's why I named you Takara, it means treasure."

I wake up and my cheeks are wet with tears. Feeling awkward, I don't open my eyes. I hold Riku and cry into his neck. My right hand rests on his chest where his heart is. Even though we are strangers he is a comfort to me. Now that I'm awake I notice how cool his hands are on my legs. He stops walking and I hear Hanako's voice.

"Do you see something, Riku?"

"No, it's Aiya. She cries in her sleep," he answers.

I don't dare let them know I'm awake.

"Aiya puts on a brave face but she carries a lot of hurt," says Hanako.

Riku resumes walking. Both of them travel like spirits with feet that never touch the ground. I wonder what he's thinking about. Hanako continues, "The first time I saw Aiya, I was mesmerized by her. I thought she must be very courageous to come out this far. I was curious why such a pretty girl would be in the middle of the forest and I followed her. After she sensed my presence she threw a rock at me! It's a funny story now that I think about it," she laughs her bubbly laugh.

"I heard someone calling my name. I got there just in time, Aiya was being attacked by a horde of nightbiters. They ambushed her and she fell off the cliff. She didn't cry then," says Riku.

"I'm glad you found her," says Hanako in a slow considerate voice.

"Me too," he replies.

***

We're close enough to the village that the demonic aura is visible. Nothing moves or makes a sound. It's dead quiet. My hand squeezes Hanako's as we approach. The fog hangs in the air unmoved by the wind. Hanako's nose wrinkles as she sniffs and her ears twitch. Riku is alert but unalarmed. Fear is absent from his face. I still can't believe he's real.

"Stay here." He motions for us to stop. He is about to enter the village but I call for him.

"Riku!"

"What is it, Aiya?" he asks.

"I just wanted to say thank you." Without words he disappears into the fog. Hanako pulls me close.

"What happens now?" she asks.

"We wait," I say.

Clinging to each other we stare into the mist. It reeks of sulfur and rot. I pray that I am not too late. How I long to see Chiyo again. Hanako's ears stick straight up and her eyes widen.

"What is it, Hanako?"

"Aiya, do you feel that?" Now that she mentions it, I hear a low rumble beyond the fog. The earth shifts and it sounds like something is shattering.

"Is it the centipede?"

"No. I think it's Riku," she answers.

We peer into the mist that begins to disperse. In the middle of the demonic clouds is a bright white light. It's getting bigger. As it grows the fog lifts away revealing parts of the village. The light is blinding and we have to shield our eyes from its brilliance. Rocks loosen and slide through the dirt. I uncover my eyes and I am in awe. Riku towers over the village in the form of a colossal white wolf. He lets out a violent roar waking the centipede.

"Go away you mangy mutt," the centipede hisses as it lunges at Riku's throat. He dodges it and knocks its face into the dirt with his massive paw. The earth moves as the centipede unwraps its monstrous body from the village.

"You want to play? Then die!" yells the centipede as it flings Riku off him.

Its serrated legs dig into the dirt and tear up the grass. It has dislodged its enormous body. It elongates itself and it stands so tall it's face to face with Riku. He paces around the demon, dodging the centipede's strikes. It lunges at Riku again, this time hitting him in the nose. He lets out a yelp in pain. The centipede's antenna bounces as it cackles.

"Bad dog," it taunts.

This enrages Riku and his eyes glow red like the other demons I have seen. He charges at the centipede and bites into the trunk of the creature with his sharp teeth. It screeches in agony. Running in circles around the centipede he begins hacking it into pieces with his massive jaws.

"What are you doing? No!" wails the centipede.

The beast tries to lift himself up but it's missing too much of its body. Riku continues shredding up the creature. The legs squirm, dripping black ink. They go limp and evaporate into the air. Riku crushes the centipede's face into the ground and rips out its throat, flinging blood throughout the tops of the trees.

The centipede lets out one last sigh. It ceases to move. Black and purple mist expel from the body of the beast as it deflates. Riku uses his jaws to pull the remaining pieces of the creature away from the village before returning to his human form.

"He's amazing," I say in a hushed tone to Hanako. She nods to agree.

"Riku is in love with you," she announces.

"How would you know?" I raise my eyebrow at her.

"I just know these sorts of things," she says in a rush. Riku is nearing us. I look up at him and feel my heart burst. The wind picks up and moves through his hair. He is stunning even though his face is covered in blood. Hanako helps me up and we walk closer to the village.

"Do you want to go in?" she asks me.

"No, I want to wait. Just a little longer." Riku stands next to me.

This time closer than usual. We observe the village in silence. I'm afraid to see who I lost yet I need to know who is still alive. As I am gathering the courage to enter I see a figure coming out to greet us. It's

Brother Minoru! He appears to have just woken up.

After rubbing his face in confusion he notices us. We lock eyes and he turns to look at Riku. The creases in his forehead soften with understanding and tears form in his lash line. Brother Minoru falls to his knees and gives Riku a gracious bow. Then I see Lady Kiyori and six of the priestesses. Sumire isn't with them. Lady Kiyori stares at Riku and her tense expression relaxes. She offers me an apologetic smile and kneels with Brother Minoru.

"Aiya! Aiya!" her voice rings out like a bell.

"Chiyo!"

She runs at lightning speed. Her slender fingers run through my hair and she buries her face in my neck. I hold her tight and she stops shaking but not before looking up at Riku.

"Aiya, it's him," she says more to herself than to me.

"His name is Riku," I tell her.

"Thank you, Riku," she says and steps away to kneel with the others.

Everyone is bowing. More and more people exit the village to gawk at us and lay their heads down. They sing his name.

"Riku, you did it. You saved them," I say.

He is looking at the crowd of people bowing and cheering. Blood drips from his chin landing at his boots but he is glorious. I'm staring into the face of our savior.

"I did it for you," he says and I know he is sincere.

***

Riku stays to help us rebuild the village. We're getting ready for the celebration tonight. Chiyo has been by my side since I got back. Sitting on a tree stump we watch Riku help the men repair the houses and shops. Everyone stares at him but he doesn't seem to mind. I think we are all captivated by him and the quiet way he cared.

"I'm sorry I didn't believe you, Aiya."

"It's okay, Chiyo. Don't worry about it," I say and put my arm around her.

"He's beautiful," she says and her face flushes.

"He is," I agree. Riku has the likeness of a god. Natsume, Hiromi, and Daina bring the men food and water. They have tried to be on their best behavior around Riku but can't help but be themselves.

"Can I touch your hair?" asks Hiromi. To our surprise Riku allows her to lift his bangs from his face.

"Look at him! He's gorgeous!" screams Daina.

"Ladies! Control yourselves." Natsume scolds them.

"It's okay," says Riku.

"His voice is to die for, too," says Hiromi.

"He's dashing!" shrieks Daina.

They almost faint but Natsume grabs the back of their kimonos and drags them away. Chiyo and I cover our mouths but can't stop giggling. Many children were missing a parent or a sibling. To cheer them up Hanako plays games and sings. They chase her and she lets her fox magic shine.

With her special powers their toys come to life one by one. She makes it rain stardust and creates a whirl of dancing petals. Spectacular shadow puppets help them smile again. They listen eagerly to the fox princess as she tells them stories. They lay in her lap and caress her ears. Hanako is happy because everyone thanked her for making the children feel safe. I think they remind her of the little ones she played with when she was young.

Brother Minoru and Lady Kiyori walk by in a relaxed fashion. They wave to me and Chiyo before bowing to Riku in passing. Lady Kiyori looks at me a moment longer. I think she still feels bad about not believing me. Even she can't resist pausing an extra moment in Riku's presence.

"We should get ready for the celebration," suggests Chiyo as she stretches her arms and yawns.

"I'll be there in a moment," I say.

"Okay, don't take too long! I need you to do my hair," she says, skipping down the path to our neighborhood.

I make my way to where the men and Riku are. The brothers and husbands of the village are enjoying their afternoon break sitting in the grass. Riku remains standing but leans against one of the few oak trees that survived the centipede's thrashing.

"Will you be at the celebration tonight?" I ask. It's cooler in the shade but my face is feverish.

"Will you be there?"

"Yes." My voice is small.

"Then I will be there," he says.

I take two steps away before I look over my shoulder to smile and wave. I wonder if what Hanako said could be true. Riku is difficult to read. Perhaps demons have a certain understanding of one another. I know he has a good heart. Hanako was right about that. I go to Chiyo's and find her trying to decide which kimono to wear. Chiyo can take hours to decide what color is perfect for an occasion.

"What do you think, Aiya?"

"I like the lavender one," I answer.

As I say the word I think of Sumire. She didn't make it. The color purple also reminds me of Hajime. His father Tetsuma was lost to the centipede as well. I remind myself to give him my condolences.

"Me too! But would the orange one be better for a celebration? Lavender might be too delicate."

"I think both look great on you," I say.

"Oh, before I forget. Here." She pulls out a kimono the color of roses. There are intricate designs stitched around the neckline and sleeves. The obi is silky snow.

"It was my mom's. I want you to have it." Chiyo holds it out to me with care.

"I can't accept this, Chiyo. It's too much," I say.

"Please, it would make me happy to see you wear it. C'mon, try it on!" She pushes it into my arm.

"Are you sure?" I ask. Chiyo's mother died of illness before I arrived in the village. I never had the pleasure of meeting her.

"Yes, of course!" she beams.

Her smile is contagious. After much discussion Chiyo decides on the lavender one. I try on the rose kimono and it fits me perfectly. Chiyo ties my obi and I do her hair. Brushing the shoulder length locks smooth and pulling them up I secure the bun and put in her favorite comb, the one with a seashell. My hair hangs to my waist and with Chiyo's help we manage to gather it all into an acceptable updo. She frames my face with two pieces of hair and adds the red spider lily hair sticks.

"You look beautiful," she sighs.

"You do as well," I say.

"Hey! Are you two ready?"

Hanako has come to retrieve us. She looks vibrant in her new kimono that accents her red and black ears. Natsume styled her dazzling starlight tresses and adorned it with beaded hair sticks.

"You look amazing!" Chiyo exclaims.

"We all do! Let's go," says Hanako waving us out the door. We link elbows with me in the middle and giggle like children the whole way there.

The torches are being lit and the music is starting. Delicious smelling food travels through the village. As we approach I see Hajime standing off to the side. My arms go slack and I pull away from Chiyo and Hanako.

"I'll be right back," I say. Trying to swallow the lump in my throat I make my way over to him. He's turned away from the celebration.

"Hajime?"

"Yes?" he steps forward to face me.

"I wanted to see how you were doing," I say.

"I'm okay. The shop won't be the same without him but me and my brothers will continue our family's craft," he says. I pull the knife he made from my kimono and hand it to him.

"No, Aiya. I want you to keep it," he says, pushing it back into my hands.

"He always made such beautiful pieces. I never knew a weapon could be a work of art until I saw your father's swordsmith shop." My voice is flooding with sorrow.

"Tetsuma was an artist first and a swordsmith second. At least that's what he would say." Hajime wipes a tear from his eye.

"I'm sorry for your loss. Tetsuma was a respected and important member of the community. I wish I got back sooner." In my stomach the pangs of guilt twist like a dagger.

"It's not your fault. You risked your life to find Riku. You saved us. I could never blame you," replies Hajime.

The music gets louder and we can hear people cheering. Chiyo and Hanako are already spinning each other around. I don't see Riku anywhere. He probably changed his mind. Hajime looks at the stars and the cool breeze moves through his dark hair.

"Hajime, would you dance with me?" I ask, holding out my hand.

"If you insist," he says.

We walk over to Hanako and Chiyo. Natsume, Hiromi, and Daina arrive and join us in the festivities. Something in me felt new, not just my hair or my clothes. Before I would have never asked someone to dance or touch another with nonchalance. My bracelet taps my wrist with the beat of the song.

Hajime is quite good at dancing. I know he wants to marry me but tonight is the first time I see Hajime as my friend, someone I enjoy being myself with. His hands are rough and full of heat unlike Riku's whose hands are perpetually cool. He twirls me and gives me away to Chiyo. She jumps and sings to the music. Her voice compliments the song and she doesn't let go until Hanako steals me. Chiyo opens her mouth in mock surprise and they both giggle before she runs off to dance with Natsume.

We have grilled fish with soup and rice. Brother Minoru and Kiyori are tending to the food. Three of the priestesses pass out bowls and chopsticks. Everything is simple but tastes better than anything I've ever eaten.

"Brother Minoru, Lady Kiyori, would you like some help?" I ask.

"We are fine, dear. Thank you," answers Brother Minoru. I see Lady Kiyori and the priestesses look at the others dancing and I get an idea.

"Let us worry about the food for a while. You all deserve to dance and have fun," I say as I move Brother Minoru away from the dishes.

"You have already done too much," says Lady Kiyori but I'm not listening.

"We'll all help. Go! Go celebrate," Hanako says as she nudges the priestesses towards the party.

Chiyo, Hanako, Hajime, and I take over and I spy glimpses of Brother Minoru moving his arms and legs in a way that reminds me of a crane, graceful and calm. One of the younger priestesses takes Lady Kiyori's hands and spins her around. I don't think I've seen Lady Kiyori look as light and free as she does right now. I scan the village for Riku but no sign of him. The priestesses return to take over and Hajime asks if I would like to dance again.

"Sure," I say and we make our way back to the music.

It's a slow romantic song this time. Many of the couples that didn't dance earlier join in around us. Hajime puts his hand in mine and his arm around my waist. At first I feel awkward but my new found friendship with Hajime eases me.

I see Yuta dancing with a young woman named Haru. They look at peace in each other's arms. The reason Yuta was sulky before is because he pined for her but had no courage to tell her. After the centipede was vanquished he proposed right away. Chiyo was overjoyed, Yuta's sour mood was cured, and another would be joining their small family. The music is fading and as my eyes drift around the crowd I see him. Hajime lets me go and looks in his direction.

"Go to him, Aiya. I know he is the one you love," he says. I open my mouth to argue but he is right. I haven't told anyone, not even myself. We nod at each other and I let his palm fall from mine.

"Can I have this dance?" I ask.

"I'm not really one to dance," says Riku.

"Just this once then," I say and take him by the crook of his arm.

He doesn't reject me and upon our arrival the band misses a beat before looking to one another and playing a high tempo song. Riku says he isn't one for dancing but he is smooth and elegant. The torches and moonlight cast shadows on his handsome face and for the first time since we met I saw him smile.

CHAPTER EIGHTEEN

The Chains that Break

We are splashing water at each other in the estuary. Her smile is accentuated by a missing tooth.

"Look!" she shouts. It's a heron with piercing red eyes. The bird is magnificent, taller than me or my sister, and all black. I've never seen an all black heron.

"Let's chase it!" says my sister.

"Emi! Wait, don't go!"

I try to stop her but she breaks from my grasp. They are running towards the sun and it blocks my vision. The tuberous roots of the water plants tangle around my ankles as I call for her. I hear the cawing of crows, their harsh voices ring in my ears. The once bright sunny day is going dark. A thousand black birds block out the sun.

"Emi, come back," I cry.

She stops running. The brackish water turns bright red and swirls around her knees. Emi is standing still but I can't seem to get any closer to her. The flowers begin to rot and die, their heads falling off in quick succession. The roots creep up my legs and hold me in place. The waxy vines dig into my thighs and leave indentations.

"Emi," I choke out her name.

Emi's blood is in the wetlands turning everything the color of fire. The sky is an orange haze. She turns around and she is missing her face. The front of her kimono is drenched, blood dripping from the hem. I want to run away but I can't.

She falls into the water igniting more crimson ripples. The black heron steps over her. In its mouth hangs something pale. The ruby eyes are familiar to me but I can't recall where I've seen them. It takes slow and calculated steps towards me. The vines are around my wrists and moving up my arms. Another one slithers across my collar bone and enters my kimono.

The bird is as tall as a man. I refuse to look up at it and stare into the red and orange mist. It looms over me and I grow cold in its shadow. As it lowers its neck we are eye to eye. In the beak of the black heron is my sister's face. I scream and thrash. The screaming sounds like it's coming from someone else but it's me. It's my voice calling for Emi.

"Soon," says the heron.

I wake up with my hairline soaked in sweat. My sister, I haven't dreamt of Emi and the black heron before. The nightmares are different. I used to see the same scene: my father dying, Kasai's shadow, and Riku's face. Now they torment me with their illusions. Since Riku stays near the village I haven't felt afraid but I should be. I know Kasai will come for me. Hanako said she led him far to the south but he travels with haste. I can't afford to forget his determination. I wash my face and brush my hair. Looking at my freckles I think of my sister.

"This is us. Two sisters, one soul."

"I wish you were," I whisper to myself.

Her face was similar to mine but she had no freckles and smiled more. To rid myself of the immeasurable sadness I make my way to the meadow where the wisteria trees grow. Retreating back into old habits I search for solace in my own company. I manage to make my way past the neighboring houses and up to the path unseen. There are bird songs and chirping insects but I hear only the wind as I run like I can escape Kasai.

My father gave me tea to make me fall asleep, then hid me in the hollow of the tree, and covered me with leaves. He defied him and Kasai set the village on fire. How could he do that to my mother? She would do anything for him. Why did he betray us all? The day he died, I stopped living. If he was alive would he even apologize? I could forgive him for what he did to me but I resent him for what he did to our family. He let Kasai destroy the whole village but I still miss him. I wish he didn't die a coward.

The purple and white petals hang over me like clouds. I find a semi sunny patch to sit and think. I pull my kimono over my knees exposing my skin to the sun. My hands rest in the grass where the light has been. They're icy in the summer heat. I can't stop shivering. I should have worn a coat. Holding my fingertips to my lips I blow on them to warm them up and wrap my arms around myself. I remember the vine in my kimono and shudder.

"Are you cold?" Riku puts his cloak around me. It smells like pine needles and ice. The fragrance reminds me of the night we met.

"Thank you," I say.

"Is something wrong?" he asks.

"It's Kasai. He's coming for me. I know he will be here soon," I reply as I pluck at the grass.

"I won't let him take you," Riku assures me.

"You've done so much for me. I don't know how I could ever repay you."

"You have done enough."

"How?" I ask. He catches me off guard with his sudden embrace and rests his chin on the top of my head.

"By being alive," he answers.

***

To prepare for Yuta and Haru's wedding I collect the white flowers that grow right outside the village. I intend to turn them into flower crowns for Chiyo and Haru. Both of them were beyond themselves with glee. It's a strange delight to see Yuta's face match his twin sister's. I think about Riku's smile and how striking it was. For someone who prefers to be alone I think he felt a sense of belonging that night at the celebration. We both did. I'm singing to myself as I pick the flowers, careful not to shake the petals loose.

It's you, it's you
The man from my dreams
The one I that I love
The reason why I sing
It's you, it's you
I've been waiting
To see

* * *

I have at least three dozen of them in my basket and I lose track of time.

> *It's you, it's you*
> *Who left me by the spring*
> *The one that I love*
> *The only reason why I sing*
> *I knew I loved you too much*
> *For it to be a dream*

I hear someone call my name. I look up to see Riku running towards me. I smile and wave at him. As he gets closer I see the panic in his gold eyes. Before I turn around I know he's there.

"There you are, Katan."

"Kasai."

"That was a dirty trick your fox friend pulled. I'll have to punish her."

His voice is lilting. He removes the head of the bear and exposes his face. The smirk he wears is wicked and malicious.

"Leave her alone!" I shout.

"Aiya!" Riku calls for me but as he nears Kasai surrounds us in his fire barrier.

"Lover boy can't save you now," he growls. Riku is attempting to cut through the barrier but it's impenetrable. He's calling my name but it's quieter now. I can't hear over the roaring flames that grow with Kasai's unrestrained laughter.

"You want me, Kasai? Then come for me!" I tempt him. In an instant he closes the gap between us. He towers over me, leaving me in his shadow.

"Riku can't break the deal, Katan. You're mine." His tongue slithers over his teeth as he talks.

"I can break my own curse," I say as I drive the knife Hajime gave me into Kasai's chest.

To my horror it barely goes in an inch. Kasai's body is made of rock. The knife jiggles with the rise and fall of his lungs as he lets out a howl of amusement.

"I don't think so," he hisses in my ear before reaching into my chest and wrapping his claws around my heart. When I die I don't feel any pain.

Mother and I are having tea as usual. Her light blue kimono spills across the floor. We are having jasmine green tea, our favorite. The herbal aroma is soft and sweet. The liquid is too hot and I blot my mouth with my sleeve. Blood, why is there blood in my mouth? I look into my cup and see it has turned thick and red. This startles me and the teacup shatters slowly as it hits the ground.

"Mother, don't drink this!" I cry but she doesn't respond.

Her face is gone but she continues to raise the teacup to her nonexistent mouth. The blood pours over the front of her kimono staining it purple like a wound.

"Who are you?" I ask.

I can't remember her name. Who am I? I wonder what my name is. How could I forget?

"Your name is Katan."

The walls are talking. They heave and sigh like a ribcage. I leave the house and see my father and Emi. I wave to them but their faces disappear. They held such importance to me just a minute ago. Why can't I recall their names? My name is Katan. Who gave me that name?

It's faint, almost inaudible, but I can hear another name being called. A man's voice, he's saying the name "Aiya." Who is Aiya? Walking through the village all I see are faceless beings. The shops are familiar but I don't know how I know them. Everything is red and orange. All the silk at the seamstress shop are shades of sunset.

The soup someone is stirring is thick crimson and the fish being grilled are the beautiful orange koi. I look into the fields where the rice grows and the grains of scarlet stand out against the green grass. It's raining in reverse, ruby water evaporating into the sky. The bracelet on my wrist is gold, it reads "Katan." That must be who I am.

"Aiya!" I hear the sonorous voice again. Scanning the crowd I look for the person calling for Aiya. I wonder if she's lost.

"Aiya, don't give in to him!"

I turn around but no one seems to be distressed. I keep walking through the village and I see a wooden toy on the ground, a spinning top. I pick it up and examine it. The name "Takara" is carved into the bottom. A child must have dropped it. I hear a baby crying in the distance. Perhaps that is the little one who lost this. I search for him but no one with a baby in their arms is here. The sky turns dark and thunderous. The lightning strikes and with it I hear it say "Katan, Katan."

Taking the spinning top with me I return to the house. The woman with no face isn't here anymore. I keep forgetting the toy in my hand but when I look at it I feel a twinge in my chest. Who did this toy belong to? Who is Takara? The lightning strikes outside the door and I jolt. A baby is crying in the corner and I kneel down to pick him up. I expect this child to have no face but to my astonishment he does! His big eyes are dark and his cheeks are fat with youth and innocence.

"Takara?" I ask. He lets out a giggle and kicks his feet.

"You're my baby brother," I whisper. I remember him. We rub noses and I'm relieved to have found my sibling.

"Takara, where have you been? I've been looking everywhere for you," I coo at him. In the blink of an eye his face is gone.

"No! Takara, please come back to me!" His face returns and he wiggles his tiny arms and legs.

"I could never forget you. My sweet boy." I press my forehead to his and we stay like that for a while.

"Aiya!" It's that voice again. It's getting louder.

"Aiya! I'm right here," it says. Then I remember. I remember everything.

I open my eyes to see the look of terror on Kasai's face.

"No! Katan!" he screams. I can feel the knife sinking deeper into his chest.

"My name is Aiya," I whisper.

"What is that, Katan? What are you doing?"

"My name is Aiya."

"Katan, please. Stop this."

His hand is on my wrist but he can't remove the knife. I'm leaning into him, bracing myself with the knife in my right hand, and my left hand on his shoulder. I pull the fur of the bear until my knuckles turn white and my blood is acidic.

"His name is Takara and you will never take him away from me!" I shout as I plunge the rest of the knife into his heart.

"Katan! No!" he screams.

"I told you my name is Aiya!"

The blade glows white in my hand as Kasai's wound seeps purple and black tar. The barrier is disappearing. Riku makes his way towards me. It was his voice that beckoned me back from that place between nightmares and reality. Kasai's flesh disintegrates like the centipede. The purple and black mist dissipates and all that's left is the bear fur that he wore.

"Aiya!" Riku calls my name but my vision goes black before he can reach me.

***

"She's coming to," says Hanako.

"Aiya, can you hear me?" It's Chiyo.

"Give her some room," instructs Lady Kiyori.

I open my eyes but everything is blurry. My head is a swollen melon balancing on my neck. Remembering Kasai's grip on my heart I reach for my chest. There is nothing there, no mark or scar. He didn't take it.

I let the wave of relief wash over me but I notice something strange. My hands, they look like Hanako's hands. I blink a few times and shake my head. No, they are definitely my hands. Still slender and petite but now adorned with sharp claws.

"Aiya, you're okay!" Hanako cheers and wraps her arms around me.

"Yeah, I'm fine. I feel weird though," I say and as soon as the words leave my lips I see Hanako's ears turn downward and her expression change.

"Here, drink this. It will help you feel better," says Lady Kiyori in a motherly tone. She hands me something cool and minty.

"My hands, why do my hands look like this?" I rasp.

Lady Kiyori pushes the cup to my mouth and urges me to drink more. She looks to Chiyo who gets up to retrieve a mirror.

"Aiya, I want you to know that no matter what I love you. You're my best friend and nothing will ever change that. Okay?" she says as she sits in front of me.

"Chiyo, what's wrong?" I feel the panic rise up in me but keep my composure.

"Nothing is wrong. Something is just...different," says Lady

Kiyori.

"Show me," I demand.

Hanako sits behind me and puts her hands on my arms. Her starlight hair falls onto my shoulder. Chiyo lifts the mirror with great reluctance. I shriek in shock at my face that's unchanged but my eyes are now blood red.

"What? What happened to me?" I stammer.

"I'm sorry Aiya. I should have warned you," says Hanako with tears in her eyes.

"Warn me of what, Hanako?" I ask.

"During the time I tricked Kasai and pretended to be you he shouted vile things. I was glad you didn't have to hear them. He planned to take your memories away so all you would have is him. He was going to turn you into a demon and take you back to The Underworld as his bride," she answers.

I knew Kasai had planned to collect me but I hadn't thought about what would happen after. Perhaps I wanted to block it out of my mind.

"It's alright, Aiya. You are still you," Lady Kiyori reassures me but I'm days away.

Chiyo takes my hand and strokes my wrist like when we were kids. My claws are out of place in her small palm.

"I need to get out of here," I say and dart out the door.

"Wait! Aiya, come back!"

Chiyo keeps calling my name but I don't turn around. I am crawling out of my skin. My body isn't mine anymore. It's been violated. I am a ruined girl. Detached from my soul with red eyes I sprint into the forest like a wild animal. With newly acquired vision I can see in the dark. The forest spirits appear to me. I've never seen them do that before. They line the path I'm on and watch me from the trees. They show no fear. I am one of them now.

The scratching legs of insects and night flowers blooming echoes in my ears. Everything is immense, even the buzz of a fly. I can hear the wings scrape together and scales fall off. There are demons in the forest but they do not approach me. They must sense I'm not human, not anymore. To test my skill I jump to a high branch in a tree with ease. I fly through the woods without breaking a sweat.

I don't know where I'm going but I end up at Brother Minoru's. Everyone is asleep in their homes, I can hear them snoring. With quiet creeping steps I make my way to Brother Minoru's door and knock twice. His body shifts and he lets out a confused sigh. As he opens the door he's rubbing his face.

"Aiya, what are you doing at this hour?" asks Brother Minoru as he looks back and forth.

I give him no words but look up at him with glowing eyes. He recoils at first but then lets me in. Lighting the fire for tea he motions for me to sit across from him.

"I heard about the fire demon," Brother Minoru starts but I interrupt him with violent sobs that rattle through my core.

"Please, tell me everything," he says and positions himself in a pious manner.

Much to my chagrin I cry through my secrets. I tell him everything. I've never confided in him like this. Through forceful tears I tell the whole story about my father's weakness, the deal with Kasai, the nightmares, and even the truth about my love for Riku. As I finish speaking Brother Minoru sits with his eyes closed. His hand rests on his chin and I wonder if he fell asleep.

"You have been touched by something dark, Aiya. But being touched by something dark doesn't mean we must succumb to darkness," he says. The small light between us illuminates only a portion of our faces.

"I'm a demon now. Part of him is inside me forever," I lament.

"You may carry him with you but don't let it be heavy," says Brother Minoru.

"Now I look into my eyes and I see him. Right here," I say and touch my chest. My heart beats below my palm and I am grateful it doesn't belong to him.

"Try to find the grain of sugar in the pile of salt," he offers. I'm growing tired of his riddles.

"What do you mean, Brother Minoru?"

"When you went into the forest in search of help, wasn't it Hanako who protected and guided you?"

"Yes," I answer.

"When you first came to our village you missed your family and were quite depressed but it was Chiyo who offered you kindness and friendship, didn't she?"

"Yes, she did."

"When you asked Riku for help, did he hesitate?"

"No, of course not." I put my hand to my shoulder and my chin down feeling ashamed.

"Perhaps this was meant to be." Brother Minoru is smiling that impish grin again.

"What do you mean?"

"Demons and humans live in different worlds. They can live for thousands of years. Now you and Riku could truly be together," he says and I am impressed by his profound suggestion. The monk didn't speak riddles after all.

CHAPTER NINETEEN

Tender is the Heart

As soon as the sun begins to rise I head to Hajime's house. I stand outside for far too long before I have the nerve to knock. The day is new and there isn't very much light. Hajime comes to the door with a crumpled face.

"Aiya, what are you doing here so early?" he asks as he runs hands through his hair several times. I look up at him with those unnatural red eyes. Like Brother Minoru he pulls back for a moment but quickly relaxes his shoulders. He puts his large hands around my face.

"What happened to you?" he asks in a whisper.

"Hajime, you said the knife you gave me had special properties. What did you mean?" I answer with my own question.

"We coat the steel with clay and ash in between folds. Normally we use straw ash but I made yours different. I took a lock of my own hair and threw it in the fire," he replies.

Hajime's love and sacrifice protected me. He put a part of himself in that weapon. I wrap my arms around his stiff body.

"You saved my life, Hajime. I was to be collected by the fire demon Kasai, a curse put on me by my father. He almost had me but I was able to kill him using the knife you gave me. I think it brought me back from the dead," I tell him. I can feel him shudder and I let go.

"You're a demon now," he says with a flat voice.

"I am. I was able to stop Kasai from taking control of my mind but

I didn't stop the transformation in time," I say as I stare at the ground.

"You are still beautiful. Demon, human, you have always been so beautiful," says Hajime.

"Thank you," I say. I wish I could offer him more.

"Will you stay here in the village? Or will you and Riku live out there with the other spirits of the forest?" asks Hajime in a considerate tone.

"I'm not sure. For a long time I felt like I didn't belong here. That I had no family. On my journey to find Riku I realized the value of what I had but I didn't appreciate it until it was too late," I admit.

"If you ask me, your family has grown. Hanako and Riku will never leave your side. I know you don't love me the way you love Riku but I am here for you, too. I hope you don't feel alone anymore, Aiya." I think over what he said and smile to myself.

"No, I don't."

I leave and go back to the field where the white flowers grow. The ones I was picking for Yuta and Haru's wedding. The hillside where I fought Kasai has a large black spot on it from the fire. I kneel down to touch the burnt grass and dead flowers. Something happened here. I clutch my chest feeling his claws wrap around my heart.

"Aiya," says Riku. His voice is sad.

"Riku, I was just looking for you," I say as I stand up.

"I'm sorry. I feel like I failed you."

"You have never failed me," I reply. He takes my hand and studies my claws that are similar to his and Hanako's.

"What happened to you in the fire barrier?" he asks.

"Kasai tried to rip out my heart and erase my memories. I stabbed him in the chest with this," I say and show him the knife Hajime made me.

"How did you defeat him?" Riku seems perplexed.

"He tried to make me forget my baby brother, Takara. It didn't work though. I'll always remember him. Even if I forget myself," I answer.

We both turn to the rising sun that paints the horizon pink, orange, and yellow. Before the sky turns blue Riku surprises me with a kiss.

"I never want to lose you," he says.

"You won't. I'm like you now. I'm strong."

"You've always been strong. Even when you were human," he replies.

***

I show obeisance in the temple before going to the sacred spring. This is where he set me down. The grass is fuller in this spot. On my knees I reach for the water. It accepts my hand and does not burn me. Expecting to be rejected I let my fingers linger, feeling the faint pull of the springwater. How is it that I can still touch it?

"You may be a demon now but your heart is pure. That's why the water has not injured you," says Lady Kiyori. I didn't realize she was behind me.

"Lady Kiyori–" I start but I am not sure what to say.

She comes closer and sits next to me with her legs crossed. The wind moves through her white kimono and shakes the paper ribbon in her hair.

"This is where Riku left you. Right here," she says as she touches the darker shade of grass. Pushing her palm into the ground elongates her slender fingers. Dark bangs frame her remorseful face.

"I'm sorry, Aiya. I was too hard on you," she says.

"You were doing your best."

"Maybe. But I shouldn't have been so harsh. Brother Minoru and I had your best interests at heart. I hope you know that," she says without making eye contact. Lady Kiyori is staring beyond the sacred spring.

"I know," I reply.

"Brother Minoru didn't tell me he saw the demon that left you here. When he called to me I was by the shrines in the sacred grounds. I sensed I was being watched but I ignored it," she says.

"Riku chose this place for me. I think he chose it for a reason," I tell her.

"What do you think the reason was?"

"You and Brother Minoru are kind and caring people. He must have known that."

"I feel honored he entrusted your life to us," she whispers.

"I'm not sure what is to become of me," I announce.

"How so?"

"I felt like I didn't belong before. Only when it was too late did I recognize what I had. Now I am truly out of place."

"Aiya, the only one who ever thought you didn't belong was you."

"What?"

"I remember the way Chiyo clung to you after you arrived. How Brother Minoru and the priestesses were so patient with you. At fifteen you had a suitor, Hajime. You have always belonged here with us. I know we can't replace your family but we have loved you for many years," says Lady Kiyori. I've never heard her speak this way. We haven't had an informal conversation like this before.

"This must be why he chose this place," I say.

"Why's that?"

"He knew I would be loved."

CHAPTER TWENTY

Runaways

Am I a ghost? Or am I reborn? I have been everything. There were days when I thought I was alone. Other times I thought I was already dead. My father was weak but he is still dear to me. Forgiveness is for the virtuous. I do not wish to give into hatred. My feelings are complicated but they are mine to explore. I have all the time I need to figure everything out.

I have never been in love but it's breathtaking. It suffocates me. My skin has blue undertones beneath the copper and tan freckles. My heart is so full it pushes the air from my lungs. The breeze is cool and refreshing. I inhale the scent of a hundred flowers. I'm by myself in the forest sitting in the tallest cedar I could find.

The mountains to the north are shades of purple. I stare at them, eager to know everything about what happened there. The gorge to the east looks like it's made of crystals. I've never been able to see this far. There are glittering precious stones in the hills. A raven lands on the branch next to me. This one doesn't have red eyes. She has amber eyes.

"Hello."

The raven hops closer and tilts its head. Her feathers are magnificent. They catch the sun and she shines. She answers me by sitting with me and we appreciate the gorgeous view together. I put out my wrist and she studies it. Giving her another chance I reach for her. This time she lands on my forearm. The raven looks into my eyes.

We share a bond I can't explain. She is part of the forest and so am I. I thought I didn't belong anywhere but now I have two worlds to call home.

Riku and I have been getting acquainted. He doesn't speak often but is sincere when he does. We spend our time together happily. Riku is shy about it but he holds my hand. I feel alive now that he's around. He seems unsure about me most of the time but we are in love. Our union is unbreakable. We have been connected by fate. It was written in the stars.

"Hey Aiya!" Hanako is calling up to me.

"I'll be right down!" I jump and weave through the branches. Landing on my feet I feel empowered.

"Whatcha doing?" she asks. We start walking back in the direction of my village.

"Just thinking." I pick up a dandelion and send out the seeds like a message from my rosy mouth.

"About what?" Hanako's ears twitch. It's adorable and makes the corners of my lips turn up.

"How everything is different now," I sigh. My breaths are hindered. Riku is a robber and takes them but I let him.

"Do you like how things are?" She looks at me with concerned chestnut eyes. Her youthful face betrays her wise demeanor.

"I love the way things are. I'm really happy, Hanako." I pick up another dandelion. "I don't have to make any more wishes."

"Good. Riku is really happy, too." My new friend surprises me with her statement.

"Do you really think so? He is quiet and difficult to read." Nervous fingers twirl my hair and I find myself biting my lower lip.

"He loves you. I think he's loved you for a long time."

"Has he said something to you?"

"No, I can just tell." Hanako wiggles her nose at me.

"How can you tell?" We are nearing the village. My fingers hurt. My hair is in knots from playing with it.

"Trust me. He does. You don't ever have to worry about that."

I want to ask her more questions but she skips ahead of me. Hanako does a cartwheel that sways her starlight hair. I join in on her fun and we laugh until our stomachs ache.

We're exiting the treeline and coming upon the hill where Kasai changed me. I see Riku standing at the burnt grass and black flowers. His eyes hold the world. They are sad but hopeful, piercing but sympathetic, and most of all they're kind. Hanako takes my hand and we watch Riku stare into the circle that created a new me.

He doesn't notice us and we don't move. I am captivated by him. The wind lifts his wispy bangs. His cloak waves behind him with triumph. The tall grass shakes and makes crisp whipping noises. Orange and pink clouds pour over us. The sun is sinking down into its resting place.

"You and him are forever," says Hanako. Her shimmery hair is in her face. I can't see her expression.

"Him and I will never die." I smile a hundred and one smiles right as Riku looks up. He is smiling, too.

***

I make the decision to leave the village but not until after the wedding. Yuta is very affectionate and doesn't let go of his bride's hand the whole time. Her smile is entrancing, I can see why Yuta fell in love with her. Everything is decorated red and white, the colors that represent happiness and joy. We wear flower crowns of red spider lilies and white camellias. Dancing with Natsume, Hiromi, and Daina, I see them all through new eyes. Never appreciated in the moment but they were dear to me.

"Promise you'll visit me," says Chiyo.

"Of course. Our lives are intertwined. You'll never be far from my heart," I tell her.

"Don't forget us!" cries Hiromi.

"I could never forget any of you," I assure her.

"I wish you both happiness," says Hajime as he gives Riku a polite bow.

"Thank you, Hajime," says Riku, "your gift kept Aiya alive," he adds. Hajime straightens up at his words with that thoughtful grin upon his face.

"Be safe out there," he says as he returns to the celebration.

"Are you ready?" Riku asks me. I nod and we slip away from the crowd. Before we enter the forest we watch the village from the top of the hill.

"I'm glad you chose this place," I say.

"You are?" asks Riku.

"Yes. I had a wonderful life there," I reply.

"Will you be happy now?"

"I'm about to live the most extraordinary life," I answer. I've been many things: a daughter, a sister, a sacrifice, an orphan, a friend, and now a demon.

"Wait for me!" calls Hanako as she bounds through the tall grass.

As the three of us enter the woods I am resurrected. Hanako skips away to play with butterflies. The orange and black wings move their fragile bodies up and down, side to side. We glide through the forest faster than the wind. There is no noise as I step. Ghosts have no fears and leave no footprints.

"Where do you want to go?" he asks.

"Take me to the place where we first met. I know nothing from my old life will be there but I need to see it one last time."

"As you wish," he replies.

My name is Aiya. I'm the girl who broke her own curse. I thought I was no one but I am everything. I will live for centuries. I can see through the spectral plain and make friends with the spirits of the forest. The weapon I carry is made with love, the strongest force in the world. My heart was almost stolen but it belongs to the wolf who walks alone no more.

THE END

Other Fine Books by Tawnya Torres

A Silent Discovery
Heart of the Machine
The Soul Keeper's Assistant
To Know Your Name
Bloodlust